THE
FRENCHMAN'S
MISTRESS

THE FRENCHMAN'S MISTRESS

BY

KATHRYN ROSS

MILLS & BOON®

*MILLS & BOON and
MILLS & BOON with the Rose Device
are registered trademarks of the publisher.*

*First published in Great Britain 2004
Large Print edition 2005
Harlequin Mills & Boon Limited,
Eton House, 18-24 Paradise Road,
Richmond, Surrey TW9 1SR*

© Kathryn Ross 2004

ISBN 0 263 18534 6

*Set in Times Roman 16½ on 18 pt.
16-0305-49987*

*Printed and bound in Great Britain
by Antony Rowe Ltd, Chippenham, Wiltshire*

CHAPTER ONE

WHEN Caitlin had told people that she was leaving England to start a new life in Provence it had sounded glamorous and exciting. Now, as she peered out through rain that seemed to be slanting in diagonal sheets across the windscreen of her car reality started to set in. *Was this it: her dream villa, her escape route from everything that had been wrong in her life?*

In her imagination the villa had been cradled in the lush green warmth of the French countryside, painted deep ochre to blend with the surroundings, green shutters closed to protect the perfectly proportioned rooms from the full glare of the Mediterranean sun. But the reality looked nothing like her dreams. Perhaps once it had been a quaint cottage, but now it looked sad and neglected and frankly rather bleak.

Maybe she had taken a wrong turning and this was not really her house? She picked up the maps, checking the route she had taken, and then glanced again at the papers she had been given at the solicitor's office. The directions had been fairly straightforward; she didn't think she had made a mistake, and there didn't seem to be another building for miles around.

Caitlin peered out at the dilapidated building again. Daylight was beginning to fade, before it went dark she was going to have to get out and investigate. Or she could turn her car around and head for the nearest village and book into a hotel. For a moment the thought of a hot shower, fine French food and cool cotton sheets was very tempting. She had set off driving from London at four-thirty this morning; it was now almost seven in the evening and she was exhausted. But she had come this far and, as tired as she was, she would not be able to rest easily until she knew for certain if this was Villa Mirabelle…her inheritance.

She switched off the car engine and the silence was filled with the rhythmic sound of rain hitting the roof so heavily it sounded like a distant roll of thunder. The world outside was lost in a dark watery haze as the windscreen wipers stopped. Caitlin pulled up the hood of her raincoat and, taking the front door key she had been given and a torch from the glove compartment of the car, she took a deep breath and stepped out of the vehicle.

Her feet sank straight into the sodden, muddy ground making her progress towards the front door a bit like paddling through thick, syrupy treacle and her jeans beneath the blue raincoat were instantly soaked and splattered with mud. There were two steps up to the front door and she almost fell up them as the rain-drops blurred her vision. In case she had the wrong place, she knocked on the wooden door and waited to hear any movement from within, but was aware of nothing except the drumming of the rain against her waterproof coat.

With slightly shaking hands she tried her key in the enormous lock. It slipped in easily but wouldn't turn. She almost laughed aloud in relief, but before taking it out tried again, this time turning it in the opposite direction. With a sinking heart she felt the soft click of the lock opening and knew then without a shadow of doubt that she had the right place.

Disappointment prickled inside her for just a second and then she quickly brushed it away as she reminded herself how kind it had been of Murdo to leave her the cottage. She would be forever grateful to him, especially as the bequest had come at a time in her life when she had most needed it. And it had been totally unexpected. It wasn't even as if she was related to him, she had merely been his nurse. There was no reason why he should have left her a single penny, let alone a property in France with all its land.

She pushed the door open and shone her torch into the thick blackness inside. The yellow beam of light played over what looked like a lot of white sheets and it took her a moment to realise that they were dustsheets over furniture. She stepped inside out of the rain and the floorboards creaked in protest as if no one had dared to step on them for a long time. There was a light switch next to the door and she flicked it on but wasn't surprised when nothing happened. The electricity was probably turned off…that was if the place still had electricity. Leaving the door open she stepped further into the room. It smelt vaguely of lavender mixed with the damp earth smell of somewhere that hadn't been aired for a long time.

On a sideboard there were a few silver-framed photographs of people Caitlin didn't recognise. They made her realise how little she knew about her former employer. He hadn't been a man given to revealing intimate insights of his life, indeed she had only known about his land in France because from time to time he had been visited by his ex next-door neighbour, a tall dark Frenchman called Ray Pascal.

As she ran a curious eye over the photographs she suddenly picked out the familiar face of Ray amongst all the strangers. She lifted the photo and blew the dust from it.

It was obviously his wedding photograph. There was a beautiful woman by his side in a long white dress; she had dark hair and laughing eyes. Caitlin guessed it had been taken about fifteen years ago because Ray looked as if he was in his early twenties. He had been good-looking back then, she thought as she studied the photograph intently, but he had matured into a formidably handsome man—if a somewhat disagreeable one. Her eyes flicked again to the woman he had married; apparently she had died in a car crash and Ray had never got over losing her.

She had only met Ray a few times but on each occasion there had been an underlying tension between them that had unnerved her completely. She wasn't used to men looking at her with such disapproval. In fairness she supposed they had got off to a bad start. The first day she had opened the door to him she had been wearing a pair of minuscule shorts and a T-shirt and he had looked at her with a raised eyebrow when she had casually told him she was Murdo's nurse.

'Aren't you a little scantily clad for work?' he had inquired dryly.

Now, at that point she probably should have explained that in fact it was her day off and she wouldn't have been there except for an urgent phone call from Murdo telling her that he needed her. Worried about him, she had rushed straight over only to find Murdo looking better than he had in ages, sitting in the lounge, telling her that there was someone coming whom he wanted her to meet.

Consequently she hadn't been in a very good mood when she had opened that door to Ray and the note of censure in his tone had been the last straw. 'What I wear for work is between my employer and me...' she had retorted coolly, and then with a toss of her long dark hair she had marched past him out of the door. 'He's in the lounge.' She had thrown the words casually back over her shoulder. 'And tell him never to ring me like that again.'

Murdo had been infuriating sometimes, she reflected wryly as she put the photo down. For some reason during the brief period of Ray's visit last summer he had got it into his head that she and Ray would make a good couple. It had been a crazy notion, not only because they didn't even like each other, but because Caitlin was with David—had in fact been living with David for three years.

After a couple of weeks of heavy innuendos Murdo had finally come out and asked her directly if she was attracted to Ray. She remembered she had blushed wildly when she had told him that she most definitely was not. Even now she didn't know why that question had made her so hot and bothered. Murdo had found her reaction amusing. He hadn't been a man given much to laughter, at least not in the two years Caitlin had known him, but he had laughed that day, a rich, warm chuckle that had even made her grin.

'I'm in love with David,' she reminded him when he continued to laugh.

'If you say so.' Murdo grinned.

'Yes I do say so, we're engaged to be married.' She waved her diamond ring in front of his eyes.

'You've been wearing that since you first worked for me,' Murdo said dismissively. 'And you've only just set a wedding date.'

She frowned. 'I know Ray is very good-looking, Murdo, but then so does he. He is arrogant and not my type at all.' Murdo's deep blue eyes twinkled in amusement and she thought maybe it was because she was protesting too much; then she realised that they were not alone. Ray was standing behind her in the doorway of the bedroom. If ever Caitlin wished the ground would open up and swallow her it was that day.

She attempted to apologise to him later, good manners forbidding her to just leave it. So she caught him when his visit with Murdo was over and he was heading for the front door.

'I'm really sorry about…before…you know…' She had tried not to be intimidated by the steady way his dark eyes held hers. 'Murdo was winding me up and…well…I shouldn't have risen to the bait.'

'You don't need to apologise,' he said and in contrast to her he sounded completely self-assured. His lips twisted in a half smile that was slightly mocking. 'The fact is, you're not my type either.'

Then he turned, leaving her wishing she hadn't bothered to apologise.

'Why didn't you warn me he was behind me?' she asked Murdo crossly a little later.

He grinned, not at all repentant. 'I don't have many pleasures left in this life but one of them is very definitely watching the sparks that fly between you and Ray.' Then the smile faded and suddenly he grew tired of the game and became cantankerous. 'I haven't taken my medicine yet… You know how I hate being even five minutes late with it…'

Murdo hadn't been the easiest of patients she reflected now, but she was going to miss him. There had been something almost endearing about him even at his most crotchety.

'Your house is a bit of a mess, Murdo.' She spoke aloud as she looked around, her voice sounding strange in the enclosed space. 'But I appreciate the thought nevertheless.'

'You know that talking to yourself is the first sign of madness.'

The voice from behind her was so unexpected that she jumped violently and spun around, her torch unsteadily wavering over the white sheets, her heart thundering against her breast.

A man stood silhouetted against the open door and for a crazy second she thought it was Murdo returning from the grave to answer her. But the outline in the doorway was that of a more powerfully built man, he was taller, the shoulders broader.

'I wondered when you'd turn up.' His French accent was dryly amused, not at all ghostly, and suddenly very familiar.

'Ray! You scared the life out of me!' She shone her torch onto him and he held a hand up to shield his eyes from the glare. The yellow beam glinted over the raindrops in his short dark hair and she noticed he wore a heavy oilskin jacket over jeans. It was a far cry from the way he had dressed when she'd seen him in England—back then he'd always worn smart suits. 'What on earth are you doing here?' she asked, lowering the beam of light from his face.

'I was on my way up to the house and saw your car.'

'Up to the house?' She was truly mystified.

'My house.' His voice was acerbic now. 'I live about six kilometres further on up this road.'

'Oh! I didn't know... Well, I knew you lived in France, of course...' She felt flustered and confused. 'But Murdo told me you had an apartment in Paris now, so I assumed you had moved from around here.'

'I do have an apartment in Paris—I use it for work—but my home is here in the south.'

There was an edge to those words that she didn't understand. Why did she always feel out of kilter when she was talking to him? Caitlin wondered. Why did he unnerve her so much? Was he telling her that she was on his territory and she wasn't welcome?

The rain seemed to be increasing outside and a bright flash of lightning lit the room, followed a few moments later by the distant rumble of thunder. And suddenly it didn't really matter that Ray's manner was unwelcoming; at least he was another human being, and in the unknown surroundings a familiar face was reassuring. 'Well, I'm glad I'll have a neighbour I know,' she said cheerfully. 'I'll be able to pop over if I run out of sugar. That's an unexpected bonus.'

'You are not thinking of staying here…are you?'

The shocked incredulity in his voice made Caitlin hesitate; she didn't honestly know what she was going to do. The plans she had made back in England now seemed absurd. She had dreamed of turning this place into a small guest-house. A vision she had unwisely shared with a few colleagues and friends who had all delightedly assured her they wanted to be the first to book themselves in.

Caitlin cringed as she imagined the expression on their faces if they could see this property. And when word travelled around the circle of their friends and David heard…he would probably laugh. The thought of David laughing at her was almost the last straw.

He had accused her of being too impulsive when she had finished with him and his tone had been patronising. He had honestly believed that she wouldn't call the wedding off. He'd thought that she would make a token visit to her mother down in London and then return to him, her common sense restored.

And then she had inherited this house and it had been like a lifeline...

Another flash of lightning lit the room and for a second Ray had a clear view of Caitlin, dark hair bedraggled around a face that looked far too pale and eyes that shimmered intensely green.

'I'll decide what I'm going to do once I can look at the place properly in the daylight.' She angled her chin up stubbornly; she wasn't going to give up on her dream that easily.

'But you can't stay here tonight,' he continued softly.

The sudden gentleness of his tone took her aback.

'Well, I suppose I'll go down to the village and book into a hotel.'

'I don't think so.' He turned away and glanced out of the door. 'The roads further down the mountain will be flooded now. Plus I think you'll find it hard to go anywhere in your car.'

'What do you mean?' She crossed to stand beside him at the door. The sky was a forbidding shade of deep indigo lit every now and then with several jagged streaks of fork lightning that illuminated the trees on the hills with unnatural brilliance. Almost immediately the light was followed by a fierce crash of thunder that reverberated and echoed through the mountains like cannon fire.

'Flash floods come out of nowhere when the weather is like this,' Ray said matter-of-factly.

Caitlin could see for herself that water was now flowing like a river down the narrow winding road she had driven up.

'Plus you've parked your car off the road; the tyres will be stuck in the mud by now.'

Following his gaze towards her old estate car, she could see that he was right.

'I'll just have to stay here then.' She tried to sound undaunted, but truthfully the thought of staying in this house, in this storm was making her panic levels rise.

'Don't be absurd.'

The scornful remark chafed on raw nerves. 'Well, have you got a better suggestion?' She turned and looked up at him.

He didn't answer immediately and in the pause a brutal roar of thunder tore through the air again.

Then he shrugged. 'Well, I suppose you'll have to come home with me, won't you?'

It wasn't the most gracious of invitations and there was a part of Caitlin that instantly wanted to refuse out of pride and say, No, thanks, I'll be fine here. But she was too tired to pretend, so instead she inclined her head. 'Thanks, I'd appreciate that,' she said.

'And anyway, I suppose it will give us a chance to talk.'

'Talk about what?' She frowned.

For a second his features were illuminated by the lightning, the dark eyes were cool, and there was something about the rugged set of his square jaw that was unyielding.

'About Murdo leaving you this place, what else? Now let's get out of here before the roads are completely impassable and we're both stuck here for the night.'

That thought galvanised Caitlin into following him back out into the rain. Carefully she locked the door behind her and hurried down the steps.

Why did Ray want to talk about Murdo's will? she wondered as she trailed behind him. But no explanation came to mind and she pushed the question away under more pressing immediate problems. The rain was cold against her face and she realised she hadn't zipped her coat up again or put her hood up. She felt water striking straight through to her skin and dripping down her back. 'I'll just get some belongings out of my car,' she called after Ray, but he didn't seem to hear her.

As she struggled to find her overnight case in the dark amidst the chaos of her other belongings Caitlin suddenly thought about the warmth and security of her old life. The apartment she had rented with David had been in a trendy area of Manchester and they had put a lot of time and effort into the furnishings and the decoration. It had been a lovely home. Then she thought about her wedding dress, which still hung in the spare wardrobe. It had been her dream dress, yards of exquisite cream silk with tiny rosebuds around the neckline. In another couple of weeks' time she would have been Mrs Caitlin Cramer. A sudden knot formed in her throat.

Caitlin found her bag and tugged it out with some impatience. Marrying David would have been a huge mistake, she told herself fiercely. Their relationship was over and she had no regrets because he wasn't the man she had thought he was.

As she swung around she was surprised to find Ray standing behind her. He reached to take the bag from her. 'Be careful around here—it's treacherous underfoot.'

'Thanks.' She smiled at him hesitantly. She was glad he'd taken the bag from her but she wasn't going to take the hand he held out to help her. 'I'll manage…' The words were no sooner out of her mouth than she lost her balance in the mud and stumbled. Only for Ray's quick reflex action, his arm catching her around the waist, she would have been on the ground. She found herself held close against him, her body pressed against the powerful contours of his. The enforced intimacy was the strangest sensation. For a moment the cold rain beating down over them was forgotten and all she was aware of was his arm holding her securely and the warm, almost electric feeling that his closeness generated.

She extricated herself from him with a feeling of awkwardness. 'Sorry about that.' She felt breathless as she met his eyes, as if the air was knocked out of her body.

He smiled. 'I told you the ground was slippery.'

Caitlin looked away from the amused glint in his eyes. She hated it when people said I told you so. And why had she imagined it pleasurable to be close to him? He was the most irritating type of man you could wish to meet.

She walked ahead of him towards his car, picking her way with care, determined not to need any further assistance. The water on the road flooded over her shoes, penetrating inside to her feet, making them squelch as she stepped up onto the running board of his silver four-wheel drive.

'Is this really the sunny south of France?' she muttered once they were safely inside the car.

Ray smiled. 'When it rains here it usually does the job properly. That's why it's lush and beautiful.'

'Is it?' Caitlin stared out of the windscreen at the dark watery surroundings. 'I'll have to take your word for it.'

There was a certain feeling of security being inside this car, it was higher off the ground than Caitlin's and the leather interior was warm and comfortable. She watched as Ray engaged the gears before negotiating a steep turn in the road. Then as the narrow track widened their way was barred by a gate.

'This marks the boundary between your land and mine,' he said, stopping the vehicle.

'So to get to your property you have to drive through mine?' she asked frowning. 'Isn't that a bit unusual?'

'There are several entrances to my estate—this is just a back route—but I do have a right of way,' Ray muttered. 'However it is an inconvenience…and that is one of the reasons I wanted to buy Murdo's property from him last year. I made him a very generous offer, in fact, when I was visiting him in England. But then I suppose you already know all about that.'

'No.' Caitlin frowned. 'I had no idea.'

'Well, my offer was substantial, which was why I was very surprised when he turned it down and then left the place to you instead.'

Caitlin suddenly understood the barbed note in his tone. Ray had wanted Murdo's land. She shifted uncomfortably in her seat. 'His will came as a surprise to me as well.'

'Really.'

'Yes, really.' Caitlin frowned. 'I don't know what you are trying to imply but I don't much care for your tone, Ray.'

He made no reply to that, but instead got out of the car. She watched him in the beam from the headlights as he opened the five-bar gate that blocked their way.

Was he insinuating that she had somehow persuaded Murdo into leaving his house to her? The idea was abhorrent.

Caitlin didn't know why Murdo had left her his property. She had been stunned when the letter had arrived from the solicitor. But the fact that it had happened at a time when she had reached a crossroads in her life had been like a pointer sent from above and she hadn't spent a lot of time analysing it.

Yes, it was an overly generous gift, but she certainly hadn't influenced him into giving her anything. The suggestion was insulting.

Ray got back into the car and drove on through the gates. There was a tense silence between them as they continued on up the long winding road, until suddenly Caitlin couldn't stand it any longer. 'Look, I don't blame you for being a bit miffed that Murdo left his land to me instead of selling it to you. I know your friendship with him goes back years and I'm a stranger by comparison, but I assure you that the decision had nothing to do with me and I certainly didn't entice Murdo to leave me anything.'

'I never said you did,' Ray said quietly. 'Although the word entice is an interesting choice. And you were…shall we say…rather unsuitably dressed for work when I first saw you…'

Remembering the scanty top and shorts that she had been wearing when she'd answered the door that day made Caitlin's face flare with colour. 'You've completely misread the situation. That was my day off.'

'And you usually went around to Murdo's house on your day off dressed like that… did you?'

The calm question sent Caitlin's temper soaring. 'No, I did not! I was around there like that because I had been summoned urgently and I thought it was an emergency. But in fact he'd only sent for me because you were there.'

'Because I was there?' Ray sounded baffled.

'Well...yes... He had this weird idea that...' Caitlin trailed off, too embarrassed to go any further.

'Weird idea about what?' Ray glanced over at her.

She shrugged. 'Well, you must have known...he thought that...you and I would make a good couple.'

'You're not serious!' There was silence for a moment and then Ray started to laugh. The warm sound of complete amusement grated on Caitlin's nerves.

'Yes, all right, Ray, we both know it's absurd. I don't much like you and you don't like me.'

'No, in fairness I have never disliked you, Caitlin,' Ray said, shaking his head. 'I've always thought you were very attractive, in fact...for a little gold-digger.'

'Right, that's it, turn the car around,' Caitlin demanded furiously.

'Why?'

The calm question made Caitlin fizz inside like a firecracker ready to explode. 'Why? Because I would rather spend the night in a rundown house with no electricity than one more moment with you in this car, let alone the night under your roof. You are rude and and...insensitive and I absolutely detest you. That's why.'

'I'm not turning the car around,' he said, without losing a shred of his cool detachment. 'So if you want to go back to Murdo's house you'll have to walk.'

Caitlin stared out at the dark wild night lit every now and then by the bright flicker of lightning and, as much as she didn't like Ray, she decided that walking wasn't an option. 'I'll phone for a taxi, then.'

'Please yourself. But no taxi will come up here in this weather. So I think you are stuck with me for tonight.'

Caitlin's hands curved into tight fists and she felt her nails digging into her skin. 'Well,

I suppose I'll have to put up with you, then,' she muttered tightly.

'I suppose you will,' he said with a hint of amusement in his tone.

The drive turned and through the rain an impressive building came into view, its windows spilling welcoming light out into the darkness. It was the kind of château that you would see in the pages of glossy magazines, quintessentially French with fairy-tale turrets at either side of the long straight edifice. Caitlin couldn't help wondering why he was so bothered about the dilapidated house down the road when he owned this palatial spread.

He parked by the front door. 'I'll get your case. You run ahead, the door will be unlocked.'

Caitlin did as he asked and hurried through the rain, almost tumbling in through the front door as an almighty roar of thunder cracked the air. It was a relief to be out of that weather and away from the close proximity of Ray Pascal. How dared he suggest that she was some kind of gold-digger? She was still reeling with shock at the horrible accusation.

Apprehensively she glanced around at her surroundings. The house was as impressive inside as it had been outside. She was standing in a wide flagged entrance hall and through an archway she could see a stone fireplace where a log fire crackled invitingly. Drawn towards the warmth of the fire, she went into the room. It was like something out of a film set. Pale orange sofas were placed strategically at either side of the huge fireplace and a staircase led up to a wooden gallery that encircled the room. Caitlin walked over and stood with her back to the fire as she admired the antique furniture, the crystal lamps that sent out a delicate warm glow, the vases of fresh flowers, the writing bureau placed by the window.

It was a large house for one man to live in alone and Caitlin wondered fleetingly if there was a serious woman in his life. Murdo hadn't seemed to think so, but then Murdo couldn't know everything. All right Ray had been widowed in his twenties, but he was about thirty-eight now she reckoned. It was a long time for a man to be on his own.

One thing was certain: Murdo had been absolutely crazy to think she and Ray were suited.

Ray came into the house carrying her case. She watched as he put it down to hang up his jacket, muscles rippling through the thin cotton of his shirt. She was willing to bet her last penny that there was no shortage of women falling into his arms or his bed...

'Have you eaten?' he asked, turning and catching her eye.

She shook her head.

'Okay, I'll show you up to your room and you can get out of those wet things while I rummage through the kitchen and see what is in the cupboards. Unfortunately my house-keeper is having some time off so you'll have to suffer my cooking.'

'I don't want anything to eat,' she said with stiff politeness. 'So if you don't mind I think I'll just turn in.'

'Of course you want something to eat. You must be starving.' He came closer. 'I'm sorry I said I thought you were a gold-digger, okay, so can we just drop the Ms Iceberg act now?'

The casual tone of his apology did little to cool her annoyance with him. 'No, it's not okay actually,' she said stonily. 'That was a very insulting remark.'

He shrugged. 'You know you can't blame me for thinking what I did. Murdo never stopped extolling your virtues and telling me how beautiful you were. I wanted to talk to him about business and all he could talk about was you. I thought he was in love with you.'

'He was sixty-five. I'm twenty-nine,' Caitlin said rigidly.

'Your point being?' Ray enquired lightly.

'That's disgusting.'

Ray shrugged. 'You wouldn't be the first twenty-nine year old to capture an older—rich—man's heart.'

'I was engaged to be married,' Caitlin said furiously.

'Murdo made no secret of the fact that he didn't like your fiancé.'

Caitlin's heart thumped uncomfortably against her chest. She had always thought Murdo's dislike of David had been irrational—after all, he'd hardly known the guy. But in light of recent discoveries it seemed Murdo had been right all along.

'You can't blame me for wondering what was going on,' Ray said.

'That's your suspicious mind; there was nothing going on!'

Ray shrugged. 'And then of course there was the time that I overheard you reassuring him that you weren't attracted to me...'

'I wasn't reassuring him!' Caitlin spluttered angrily. 'I was telling him in no uncertain terms how absurd his notion was about us.'

Ray grinned. 'With the benefit of hindsight I can see I might have got things wrong.'

'Not might... You definitely made a big mistake,' Caitlinsaid firmly.

Ray nodded. 'Absolutely. So, now we have that cleared up, how about I take you upstairs so you can freshen up before dinner?'

Caitlin shrugged. In truth she was a bit hungry and she was longing for a hot shower. And she supposed he had apologised... 'Okay.'

'Good.' He smiled and she noticed how his eyes were almost as dark as the raven-black of his hair; there was something intensely sensual about those eyes. 'I'm glad we have sorted that out.' He reached out and, to her consternation, stroked back a stray strand of wet hair from her face.

His touch was oddly tender and as she looked up into his eyes there was a crazy moment where she felt her stomach flip as a wild rush of pure physical attraction hit her. Hastily she stepped back from him. What the heck was wrong with her? she wondered frantically. She disliked Ray...disliked him intensely.

'So, tell me, where is your fiancé?'

The sudden question was almost as disconcerting as the feeling that had just struck her.

'He's back in Manchester.'

'Well, I gathered he wasn't here,' Ray said sardonically.

A heavy rumble of thunder filled the air and the electric lights flickered.

'The storm sounds like it's directly overhead,' Caitlin said nervously.

'Yes, seems like it.' Ray turned away. 'Come on, I'll show you up to your room.'

Relieved that the subject of David had been dropped, Caitlin followed him upstairs. Ray opened a door and led her through into a large bedroom decorated in a pale shade of lemon.

'There's an *en suite* bathroom through there.' Ray waved a hand towards the other end of the room. 'Just make yourself at home.'

'Thank you.'

He nodded, seemed about to turn away then paused. 'So…you didn't tell me… Is your fiancé following you out here?'

He seemed to be looking at her very closely and she realised that, as well as being incredibly sexy, his eyes could also be disturbingly intense, as if they could reach into her very soul and find all the secrets hidden there.

She intended to tell him that her engagement was off but instead she found herself saying something completely different. 'Yes. He's just too busy with work to come over at the moment.'

'I see.' Ray smiled and she wondered if he did see…if it was entirely obvious that David would never be joining her here. 'Well, I'll leave you to freshen up. Come down when you are ready.'

Caitlin stood where she was as the door closed quietly behind him. Why had she done that? she wondered. Why had she lied?

Maybe it was just that her pride wouldn't let her admit that she had made a mistake with David. Or maybe because she felt vulnerable around Ray Pascal. She didn't know what it was, but the guy fascinated her in some strange way. He seemed to have danger written all over him.

CHAPTER TWO

THE storm was still raging outside as Caitlin finished drying her hair. She stepped back to survey her appearance in the bedroom mirror. The mud-spattered jeans had been replaced by a clean faded blue pair and a black top with a scooped neckline, not particularly glamorous apparel but at least she looked human again. Her dark hair was shining and healthy-looking, and the shower had restored some colour to her cheeks.

Her eyes flicked towards her waistband. She had lost weight. Caitlin had always been slender but now her jeans hung slightly on her waist. It was stress, probably. She had always been the same—as soon as something worried her, weight just dropped off her. And the past few weeks had been amongst the worst of her life.

The strange thing was that there had been no hint of what was to come. Everything had seemed so settled...her wedding date fixed.

Okay she'd had a few fleeting doubts about the marriage, but she had brushed them aside thinking they had just been the normal cold feet variety, the kind of uncertainties that faced most people before they made such a massive lifelong commitment.

Caitlin had thought she loved David... The only thing that had concerned her was the fact that he had never set her passions completely on fire. But as soon as those thoughts had entered her head she had always dismissed them, feeling guilty for even having given them space. Because David had seemed so easygoing and he'd made her laugh. He had been boyishly good-looking. Not as powerfully handsome as Ray, but attractive nevertheless with thick sandy-blond hair, grey eyes and a pleasing physique. Most of all she had felt safe with David. And after the disastrous relationship she'd had before him, that feeling of security had been important to her. She had been ready to start a family... Her thirtieth birthday was looming and she could feel her body clock starting to tick.

David had agreed that they would start trying for a baby straight after the wedding.

Caitlin remembered how after that discussion he had pulled her into his arms and held her tight. 'I'll make you happy, Caitlin,' he had whispered. 'I promise I will.'

There had been something of the little boy about David, she thought now; something endearing. And like her he wasn't afraid of hard work. He had a high-flying career and all the glossy accessories that went with it; a top-of-the-range sports car, expensive clothes and a taste for the high life. They'd had a good time together, meals out, trips to the races with never more than a modest flutter, a good circle of friends. There had been nothing to suggest that he wasn't the respected and responsible man that he claimed to be.

Then a few months ago he had arrived home without his car. He'd told her it had been stolen and she'd had no reason to disbelieve that. At the time she had been too worried about Murdo to give it much thought anyway. His health had been deteriorating rapidly and she'd been spending most of her spare time with him. Then she had arrived home late one night and had thought they had been burgled. The TV had gone, so had the stereo and DVD player. In fact anything of any value had just been ripped out, including personal items of jewellery. She'd been alone in the flat and terrified. David had arrived just as she'd been phoning the police.

'You don't need to do that,' he said calmly, taking the phone from her and putting it down. 'It's all under control. They have already been around here.'

Caitlin believed him. She'd had no reason not to; she trusted him.

It wasn't until later in the week when she phoned the police to see how the investigation was going that she realised David had lied to her and something was very wrong, because the burglary had never been reported.

When she went in to see Murdo that day she didn't intend on saying anything, but he caught hold of her arm as she made to leave his bed.

'So what's the matter with you?' he asked gruffly.

'Nothing.'

He didn't let go of her and his grip was surprisingly strong. 'We've always been able to talk in the past.' He'd pulled her back towards the bed and she'd sat beside him.

'It's just this burglary… David didn't report it; at least, the police say there is no record of it being reported. And when I rang him at work to ask him about it he was furious with me, said the police had made a mistake and lost the report or something. He said he'd deal with it later and I wasn't to get involved.'

She remembered the look on Murdo's face. He was frail; his skin as grey as the colour of his hair, but in those few moments there was a glimpse of his former vitality in the sudden anger of his dark eyes. 'Do you believe him?'

Caitlin shrugged and looked away from him. 'Why would he lie?'

'David may not be all that he seems,' Murdo said softly. 'I didn't tell you this, Caitlin. But a long time ago…about five months after you came to work for me, David came to collect you. There was some money sitting on the coffee table in the lounge. And when he'd gone…so had the money.' He noted the expression of horror on her face. 'I didn't tell you because I knew you'd look like that and, anyway, I'd no proof and I didn't want to risk you falling out with me.'

'How much money was it?' Caitlin asked distraught.

'The money doesn't matter.' Murdo was dismissive. 'It wasn't that much anyway... It's you I care about.' He squeezed her hand. 'If I'd had a child...a daughter...I'd have wanted her to be just like you; you know that, don't you? And I appreciate everything you have done for me—'

'Murdo, you don't need to say this,' she said tearfully.

'Yes, I do. Because the time we have together is growing short now. And I want you to know that I care about what happens to you and I want you to be happy. And, quite frankly, Caitlin, I don't think David is right for you.'

Just thinking about that conversation—one of the last conversations she'd had with Murdo—made her eyes fill with tears.

Hurriedly she brushed a hand underneath her eyes. It was strange how she and Murdo had bonded. There had been so many years between them and no blood ties, and yet when he had died it had been like losing a member of her family.

Murdo had been right about David. When she'd got back to the flat that night she had raided the cupboards and drawers to see if she could shed some light on what was going on. And that was when she had discovered the pawn tickets for their belongings and the joint credit cards that she knew nothing about. Cards with bills that she was jointly responsible for...

It had turned out that David had a serious gambling habit, although he didn't see it like that. When confronted, he had become almost violent towards her and the tone of his voice had frightened her. It had been as if he had become a stranger when he had informed her that he could do what he liked with his life, was just going through a bad patch, that if she left it to him he'd sort it out in a few weeks.

Even as she had walked out of the flat with her bags packed he had been telling her that he'd fix everything, and that she was being stupid...that it was a set-back and he'd had them before. And of course they would still get married.

If David was waiting for her to go back to him, he was going to have a very long wait.

But should she stay in France? The question churned inside her as she headed back downstairs.

Apart from the fire that still burned brightly in the stone fireplace, the lounge was in darkness.

'Ray?' Caitlin paused at the end of the stairs, wondering which way she should go.

There was no answer, only the roar of thunder and the bright flickering light of the storm illuminating the trees outside the lattice windows.

'Ray?' She wandered down the long hallway glancing through open doors at darkened rooms. Then as she rounded a corner she saw light at the end of the corridor and heard the low murmur of a radio.

'Ah, there you are.' He turned from the stove as she stepped through the doorway. 'You look better,' he said, his eyes sweeping over her.

'Well, it wasn't hard,' she said self-consciously. 'I looked dreadful before.'

'No, you didn't... You looked...' He paused, as if searching his perfect English for the exact word. 'Strained.'

'Well, I'd been driving since the early hours of this morning...and the house was a bit of a shock. Not to mention your...wild accusations—'

'Hey.' He caught hold of her arm as she walked towards him. 'I've apologised for that...so can't we just forget it?' He seemed to be looking very deeply into her eyes.

She shrugged, feeling uncomfortable again. 'Yes, I suppose so.'

'Good.' He smiled at her and she felt a surge of butterflies inside. What on earth was wrong with her? she wondered dazedly. She didn't like this man; he was arrogant, irritating and, anyway, she was off men, probably would be for the rest of her life.

Carefully she moved away from him and walked across to the stove. 'Can I do anything to help?'

'No, it's all done. I made pasta... I hope that's acceptable?'

'Very.'

'Okay, well, I'll lay the table in the dining room and we can move through.'

'Let's just eat in here, shall we?' Caitlin said quickly, not liking the thought of leaving the

warmth of this kitchen for the darkened intimacy of a dining room. There was something
reassuring about this friendly light space, the
stylish country pine décor, the Aga, and the
babble of the radio even if it was in French.

'If you like.' He shrugged.

'Shall I lay the table for you?' She pounced
as he opened a cutlery drawer. 'I may as well
make myself useful.'

'Okay.' He stepped back. 'I'll open a bottle
of wine.'

'That would be lovely.' Caitlin busied herself clearing the pine table, transferring the
vase of daisies and some post over onto a sideboard.

They sat down opposite each other at the
table. Caitlin glanced across at him apprehensively. She noticed that he had changed his
clothing since they had arrived back and was
wearing a dark shirt and dark trousers. The at-
tire was more formal and made him appear
even more intimidating for some reason.

What was it about Ray that unnerved her?
Caitlin wondered as she watched him surreptitiously from beneath dark lashes. Was it the
fact that he was able to wind her up with such

insouciant ease? Or the fact that he was over-whelmingly handsome, or was it just the whole package? There was a latent power about him, a look that magnetically drew and held the senses. Everything about him was enthralling, from the way his clothes sat so easily on his broad-shouldered frame to the fact that he was French and spoke perfect English with an accent that sent shivers of sensuality racing down a woman's spine. Then there were his eyes… His most lethal weapon, dark and penetrating, they had a way of slicing through you that could disconcert and disarm all at the same time.

As if sensing her gaze, he turned those eyes on her now. The impact was intense. It had always been the same; on their first meeting just over a year ago he'd glanced at her and her senses had reeled into chaos. That one man should be able to exert so much power over her senses had scared her then… It still did now.

He smiled, a faint, almost imperceptible light of amusement in his eyes.

'Well, I'm sure Murdo would approve of us dining here together tonight,' he said. 'So maybe we should drink to absent friends?'

'Absent friends...' Caitlin raised her glass and touched it against his.

He smiled at her and she felt that same prickle of unease that told her she had to keep her wits very firmly about her.

Hastily she looked away.

There was silence between them filled with the drumming of rain against the window and the soft melody of a French song on the radio.

She looked at the bottle of wine and noticed it had a label with the name Pascal on it. 'Is this any relation to you?' she asked, tapping the label curiously.

'It's from this estate. But I have little to do with it now. My cousin is the local wine producer; I just rent him the land.'

'It's very good.'

'Not bad.' Ray nodded. 'So how long did it take you to drive here?' he asked, switching the subject.

'I broke the journey at my mother's place in London last night. Then set off at four-thirty this morning.'

'That's a long drive. You should have flown from Manchester.'

'I wanted to bring as much of my belongings as possible. Plus it gave me a chance to see my mum before leaving.' Caitlin remembered the horrified look on her mother's face when she had told her that her relationship with David was definitely over and that she was moving to France.

'Couldn't David have driven over later with your belongings?' Ray asked.

Caitlin tried to concentrate on what he was saying and shut out the image of her mother, who had tried to persuade her to stay on in London with her to think about things. 'Do you really want to finish with David?' she had asked in some distress. 'All the invitations are out. The wedding is only weeks away. Caitlin, you are probably just suffering from nerves.'

She hadn't wanted to tell her mother that the breakup was down to something far more serious than nerves. The truth would just have been too much for her to bear. It had been better to sound upbeat and positive, as if she had made the right decision and the split had been amicable.

'Caitlin?'

'Oh, sorry.' Aware that Ray was waiting for an answer, she quickly pulled herself together. 'I suppose he could have driven over later, but as I told you earlier he's pretty busy at work right now.'

'What does he do for a living?'

Caitlin toyed with her glass. Why did he keep asking her about David? she wondered irately. 'He's in advertising.' With a determined effort she fixed him with a direct look and changed the subject. 'What about you?' she asked. 'What do you do for a living?'

'I'm an architect.'

'Oh, yes, I remember Murdo telling me now.' She smiled. 'He said you were a rare combination of creative genius and hard-headed businessman, and that you could sometimes be a bit eccentric.'

'Coming from the king of eccentricity, I'll take that as a compliment,' Ray said easily.

'Well, he was an artist and I suppose they are allowed to be eccentric,' Caitlin reflected.

Ray smiled. 'I suppose they are,' he conceded. 'His paintings are fetching tremendous sums of money, I believe.'

'Yes, so I heard.'

'He left me two in his will as a matter of fact. I haven't received them yet—they are being crated up and shipped out to me next week.'

'That was kind of him.' She looked over at Ray hesitantly. 'He seemed very fond of you.'

'He was an old family friend.' Ray shrugged. 'Best man at my parents' wedding and later when my father died he helped my mother through a difficult time.'

'I didn't realise the bond was that close.' Caitlin toyed with her wineglass. 'And yet you didn't come to his funeral?' She had looked for him on that dreadful day, had been surprisingly disappointed not to see him at the graveside.

'I was in Paris on business. I didn't know he'd died until later that week; it was too late by then.'

'I see.'

'So what are you going to do about Murdo's house?' Ray changed the subject. 'I know that inheriting it was a shock, but I'm sure the state of the place was an even bigger one.'

'Yes. I don't know what I was expecting but it wasn't…that.'

'I did try to tell him that the place had fallen into a state of disrepair, but I don't think he was listening to me.'

'He was good at that.' Caitlin smiled. 'If he didn't want to hear something he'd just blank it completely. As my grandma would have said, he had selective hearing.'

Ray laughed. 'You're right, he did.'

'And he was as cantankerous as hell sometimes...' Caitlin smiled. 'But, strange thing is, I'm really going to miss him. We grew quite close in the two years I looked after him.' She looked up at him quickly. 'Well, when I say we grew close I mean...he was like a father figure to me,' she explained quickly.

'Relax, Caitlin,' Ray said with a shake of his head. 'I think we have established that.'

'Well...I suppose I still can't get over the fact that you thought Murdo was in love with me... It's just...wild.'

Ray shrugged. 'He always did have an eye for a pretty woman.'

'He was also very ill.'

'Not too ill to try a spot of matchmaking, though?'

'He had some very strange ideas some-times,' she murmured.

'Yes, very strange,' Ray said wryly. 'I've been thinking about it and I suppose that's why he left you his house. It's a last-ditch attempt to throw us together.'

'No...I don't think so,' Caitlin said quickly.

Ray met her eyes steadily. 'Why not? It seems obvious now I think about it. Murdo always was stubbornly persistent when he got an idea into his head.'

'Even so, I don't think he would be that dogged.' Caitlin's voice was firm. She wanted to squash that suggestion in Ray's mind the way she had squashed it in her own. Even en-tertaining that idea for a moment was highly embarrassing. 'It's totally preposterous.'

'Totally.' Ray met her eyes and smiled. 'As is the thought of you living in that house. The place is uninhabitable and it will be hard work to put it right. Which is why I think it would be best all around if you sold it to me—'

'Now hold on a minute...' Caitlin cut across his sweeping statement, instantly on the defen-sive. 'I've only just arrived, Ray, and I'm hop-ing to keep the house. I like the idea of living in the French countryside and I'm no stranger to hard work.'

'I'm sure you are not. But you have to admit that the house would demand a lot of attention, you would have to organise builders and decorators and I bet neither you nor David speak French.'

'I speak some French.' She angled her chin up and met his eyes determinedly. It was one thing if she decided not to stay...quite another being told she was incapable of staying! 'And I'm very handy with a paintbrush.'

To her annoyance he seemed to find that remark amusing. 'I think you'll need a little more than a lick of paint to put that place right.'

'I'm not incapable.'

'Then there is the land...' Ray swept on as if she hadn't spoken. 'Over a hundred olive trees and a small vineyard—it all takes expertise and hard work.'

'I didn't know there was a vineyard.'

Ray nodded. 'Murdo didn't make the wine himself—he used to sell the grapes. It was a bit of a hobby for him, really.'

'I could do that,' Caitlin reflected thoughtfully.

'Now, come on, Caitlin.' Ray shook his head. 'You're not serious?'

'Why not?'

'Because, as I just said, looking after a place like that takes a certain amount of expertise.'

'I could learn.' She shrugged. 'I could do anything I set my mind to.'

'Maybe you could...' Ray said slowly, noticing the light of determination in her eyes. 'But why would you want to? You are a qualified nurse.'

'I feel like a change of direction.' She toyed with her glass of wine. Nursing had been rewarding, but recently she'd also found it exhausting both emotionally and physically. And after the trauma of her breakup with David she felt like a whole new start. 'Actually I was thinking that I could convert the...building into a small guest-house.'

For a moment Ray's eyes seemed to narrow on her. 'And what does David think about that idea?'

Caitlin frowned. Why did he keep bringing David into this? It really irritated her. 'Nothing is set in stone yet,' she said noncommittally. 'I'll have to take a closer look at the property in daylight.'

'You mean he's not too happy about it,' Ray said dryly.

She met his gaze frostily. 'This is my decision, not David's.'

'Call me old-fashioned, but I thought when you were engaged to be married you made joint decisions,' he said bluntly.

He watched the rise of colour in her cheeks and then reached to refill her wineglass. 'Sorry, it's none of my business.'

'You're right, it's not.'

For a moment Ray was silent. He ran one finger around the rim of his glass thoughtfully. 'It seems to me that the house is causing you problems already. And it's going to get worse. The place is a mess and it is certainly no place for a woman on her own.'

'You are very patronizing, do you know that?' she said quietly.

'Well, I'm sorry if you feel like that.' He looked up at her then, his eyes incisive and direct. 'But I'm just being honest. So let's cut to the bottom line, shall we? I want that land and the offer I made to Murdo is still open.'

'I haven't decided what I'm doing with the house yet, Ray. I haven't had time to think—'

'Well, let me help you think more clearly.' He cut across her impatiently and then named a sum of money that made her breath catch.

For a moment she didn't say anything, she was too stunned to make a reply.

He glanced over and met her eyes. 'It's a generous offer considering the condition of the place.'

'I'm sure it is,' she murmured, totally taken aback.

'Well, think about it.' His mouth twisted in a sudden grin. 'When you've taken a look at the place in daylight you can give me your answer.'

In other words he was quietly confident that once she had assessed the level of work needed she would take his money. Caitlin would have liked to toss her head defiantly, tell him she didn't need his money, that she was staying. She didn't like that smug attitude that said clearly that he didn't think she was up to the challenge, and she didn't like giving up so easily on her dream for a new life. But she had to be sensible. The mess of her relationship with David had left her savings sadly depleted and she didn't know if she could afford the renovations the house needed.

'Okay.' She inclined her head. 'I'll consider it. But I feel I should tell you that selling the house isn't a straightforward option.'

'Why not?'

Caitlin shrugged. 'Apparently Murdo put a few provisos in his will covering that possibility.'

'What kind of provisos?' Ray asked.

Caitlin noticed the sudden tensing of his attitude and had to smile. Ray obviously thought that throwing money about could solve any problem. But maybe he had reckoned without Murdo's steely determination. 'I don't honestly know.' She shrugged. 'I was so overwhelmed by Murdo's generous gift that I didn't pay much attention to the details. It was something about waiting six months. Or I had to live here for six months...' She shrugged. 'Something along those lines.'

Ray drummed his fingers impatiently against the table. 'Well, I suppose we'll get around all that. With the help of a good lawyer there are usually ways around most problems.'

'Maybe.' Caitlin sipped her wine and couldn't resist adding. 'But that's if I decide to sell.'

'Once you've looked at that place again I think you'll agree that I've offered a very fair price.' Ray lifted his glass in a salute.

Caitlin straightened her cutlery. She didn't feel like drinking to that toast. The thought of a new beginning in France had been all that had kept her going these past few weeks. It had been the one ray of hope in an otherwise bleak future. Going back to England didn't seem like something to feel overjoyed about.

'I haven't made any promises,' she said quietly. 'And I have to tell you I won't be rushing to find ways of breaking Murdo's will. I respected him too much for that.'

'You are obviously a woman of great integrity,' he said.

She glanced over at him, unsure if he was being facetious. 'For a gold-digger, you mean?'

His lips twisted wryly. 'I thought we'd bypassed that.'

'So did I. But your tone leaves me in some doubt.'

For a moment their eyes met across the table. There was something forceful about the way he looked at her, something that made her raise her chin slightly and defiantly. 'So as I said before…I'm not making any promises. I'm a woman who enjoys a challenge and that house might be just what I'm looking for.'

There was a flicker of some emotion in the darkness of his eyes and then a grin tugged at the sensual curve of his lips. 'I can suddenly see why Murdo might have thought that you and I would be well suited.'

'Can you?' Caitlin was taken aback by the observation. 'Why's that?'

'Because I also enjoy a challenge, Caitlin.'

Disconcerted, Caitlin looked away from him. She didn't know what to say to that.

Outside the thunder growled threateningly, filling the silence between them. The lights flickered.

Suddenly Caitlin felt as if she had endured enough for one day, she just wanted to escape to the sanctuary of her room. 'Anyway, I think I'll turn in now if you don't mind.'

'Not at all.' He picked up their empty plates and brought them over to the sink. 'Would you like a coffee before you retire?'

'No, thank you, I'm really tired.' She was just getting up from the table when her mobile phone rang. It was lying on the counter and Ray picked it up for her. 'You put it down when you were laying the table,' he said, and then glanced at the screen before handing it over. 'It's your fiancé.'

'Thanks.' She felt her heart thud with apprehension as she took the phone from him. Then as she turned from Ray's line of vision she clicked the disconnect button. There was no way she wanted to have a conversation with David tonight.

'We got cut off,' she said as Ray looked over at her inquiringly.

Before she could switch the phone off completely it rang again. 'I'll just take the call in the other room, if you don't mind.' Hastily she stepped out of the room and walked down the corridor, turning her phone's ring tone onto silent.

The lounge was still in darkness, the fire had almost burnt out—just a fragile orange glow remained. Caitlin sat down on the edge of the sofa and tried to pull herself together. Just the thought of talking to David made her feel sick inside. She couldn't face it... There was too much pain inside her...too much hurt altogether.

It was quiet in the room; the only sound was the rain against the windows. Back in her apartment in Manchester there was always a constant rumble of traffic despite the double glazing. Was that where David was sitting now as he tried to phone her? Did he regret his behaviour?

Although she was furious with him, there was a part of her that also felt sorry for him. He obviously needed help.

'Are you okay?' Ray's voice from the doorway made her strive very hurriedly to compose herself.

'Absolutely.' Her voice wobbled a little and she swallowed hard before continuing. 'Everything is fine.'

He switched on one of the lamps and looked at her, his dark eyes searching over her face.

'The weather is shocking in Manchester, apparently,' she lied cheerfully and forced herself to smile.

'I know you didn't speak to him, Caitlin,' he said calmly.

'Of course I spoke to him.' She sat ramrod straight and watched as he walked over to throw a log on the fire.

'No, you didn't, you hung up on him.' Ray stimulated the dying embers of the fire with a poker, prodding it back to life until the flames crackled greedily around the wood.

She met his eyes with a tinge of annoyance and decided to just sidestep the issue. She didn't want to talk about this and it was none of his damn business anyway. 'I don't know where you have got such strange ideas from. Now, thank you for dinner, I'm going to bed if you don't mind.'

Unfortunately as she headed for the stairs she had to walk past him and that was when he reached out and took hold of her left hand, halting her in her tracks.

'The strange ideas started when I noticed this.' She looked down and watched as he lightly traced his thumb over the white band of naked skin on her third finger. 'It's a bit of a give-away, Caitlin,' he said softly. 'I noticed it straight away over dinner. If you were my

fiancé I wouldn't want you to walk away without the symbol of our betrothal visibly in
place.'

She stared down at her finger, the finger that
had worn David's ring for three years, and a
shivery feeling raced through her, but strangely
it wasn't caused by the thought of her broken
engagement—it was caused by the way Ray
was touching her and the strange intimacy of
his tone.

She pulled away from him. 'How very ob-
servant of you.' She tried to keep her voice
brisk, but it had a quaver to it that wasn't normal. 'If you noticed it straight away, why did
you keep asking me about David?'

'Because I thought it better you tell me
about it in your own time.'

'Dear Abby eat your heart out,' Caitlin muttered sarcastically.

'Dear who?' One dark eyebrow rose. 'Who
is this Dear Abby?'

'She's an agony aunt. I was being facetious.'

Ray's lips twisted wryly. 'You don't need
to hide behind sarcasm, Caitlin, and you don't
need an agony aunt.'

'I suppose you are going to tell me what I do need now,' Caitlin murmured.

Ray reached out and put a finger under her chin, tipping her face up so that she was forced to look at him. 'You need a good friend, and in the absence of Murdo and everyone else you've left behind in England... If you need to talk, I'm a good listener.'

'I don't need to talk.' She stepped back from him because the touch of his hand against her skin was starting to do crazy things to her senses. 'I'm fine...absolutely fine.'

'If you say so.'

'I do.'

'So Murdo was right all along. David wasn't the man for you.' The steady, serious way he looked at her made the shivery feeling inside her intensify.

She looked away from him in confusion. 'Well, maybe...'

'So you must just tell yourself that you have had a lucky escape.'

Caitlin thought about all the plans and dreams she'd had for the future...about the wedding...the baby she had wanted. 'I don't feel very lucky,' she murmured huskily.

For just a second, the veil of composure slipped from Caitlin's expression and Ray saw a glimpse of vulnerability in the beautiful eyes that looked up at him. Then she pulled herself sharply up. 'Anyway, I'll wish you goodnight,' she continued on briskly.

'Goodnight, *chéri.*' His voice followed her as she moved away. 'Sweet dreams.'

CHAPTER THREE

DESPITE the fact that she was so tired, Caitlin couldn't sleep. She tossed and turned and her mind seemed to catapult from the life she had left behind to her strange new surroundings. She lay listening as the rain lashed against the window and thought about the house down the road with its crumbling walls and ramshackle rooms. Had she made a mistake coming to France?

When she finally fell asleep her dreams were a confused tangle of places and people. She could see David, his grey eyes glinting with amusement as he asked her if she really intended living in that house. 'Come home, Caitlin,' he whispered earnestly. 'Come home and we'll be married, this is madness.'

Then suddenly she was walking down a church aisle in her cream dress. She could see the scene vividly, could hear the organ playing, could even smell the scent of the roses in her bouquet. Her best friend Heidi smiled at her and waved. 'I knew it would all work out well in the end,' she whispered.

Her mother was wearing her new blue outfit with the matching wide-brimmed hat that she had searched the length and breadth of London for; she wiped a tear from her eyes as Caitlin passed. 'You look wonderful, darling; see, I told you it was just nerves.'

Then as she reached the top of the aisle she could see David waiting for her. He looked very handsome in his dark suit, hair glinting in a shaft of light shining down from one of the windows. He turned slowly and smiled at her. Only it wasn't David, it was Ray!

She woke up, her heart racing with shock, and sat up. The pretty room with its primrose-yellow walls and floral bedclothes was unfamiliar to her. Sunlight streamed through the open curtains, reflecting on the mirror of the dark wooden dressing table, and glinting into her sleep-filled eyes.

It took a moment before she realised where she was, another moment for her to realise that her heart was racing because of a dream. She lay back against the pillows and sighed. What an absurd thought! Marrying Ray indeed! Even if he were the marrying kind, which she strongly suspected he was not, he was definitely not her type.

She flung the bedclothes off and walked over to the window. The rain clouds had gone, replaced by a clear, freshly washed blue sky. A misty haze of heat shimmered over the undulating countryside criss-crossed by vineyards and lush green fields awash with crimson poppies. The scene was so beautiful that Caitlin could hardly wait to get outside. Her bad dream forgotten, she headed for the shower.

There seemed to be no one about downstairs. Caitlin went into the kitchen and put on the kettle, then stood at the kitchen sink looking across towards the purple mountains in the distance.

What would today bring? she wondered. She supposed she should ring her mother and tell her that all was well and she was safe. Where was her phone? she wondered suddenly. She didn't remember seeing it in her room this morning. Quickly she retraced her steps through to the lounge, wondering if she had left it in there last night. She was searching behind cushions when Ray came downstairs.

'Looking for this?' He held up her phone.

'Yes.' Caitlin straightened and watched as he walked across towards her.

Hell, but he was impossibly handsome, she thought. Like her, he was wearing jeans. They clung to his lithe hips and waist, and the light blue shirt he wore empha-sised the breadth of his shoulders.

She tried to avoid touching him as she took the phone back. Why she didn't know…he just made her incredibly wary.

'So, did you sleep well?'

She looked up and met his gaze and felt herself dissolve at the impact of his dark eyes.

'Yes, thanks.' She tried not to think about her crazy dream.

'Good.' He smiled and she noticed the sensual curve of his lips. 'We'll have some breakfast and go and see about your car.' He turned towards the kitchen and then glanced back. 'By, the way you've missed two calls this morning.'

'Have I?' Caitlin looked down at her phone but there was no message to say she'd missed calls.

'Yes. One from your mother, lovely woman—we had a long conversation.'

'I beg your pardon!' Caitlin hurried after him towards the kitchen. 'You mean you answered my phone?'

'Yes...well, it was sitting next to me.'

'You've got no right to answer my phone.' Caitlin was furious. 'Whoever it was could have left a message with the answer service.'

'They did leave a message...with me.' Ray seemed totally oblivious to her rage. He took some croissants from a bag by the bread bin. 'Now. I know the English like their bacon and eggs—'

'I don't want anything to eat.'

'Now, Caitlin, I promised your mother that I would keep an eye on you and that involved making sure you ate something,' Ray said calmly.

'How dare you speak to my mother—'

Ray shook his head and glanced over at her. 'She's very worried about you, you know. She thinks you have gone far too thin.' His eyes flicked down over her. 'And actually I agree with her.'

Caitlin could feel heat seeping up under her skin and she felt as if she wanted to explode. 'That is my private phone and you shouldn't have touched it.'

'So, shall I rustle up some bacon and eggs or do you just want the croissants?'

'I don't want anything.'

'We'll have the croissants, then. I have some chocolate ones here and you can go heavy on the butter if you like... I know that is an English penchant.' The smell of them mingled with the coffee he had set on the stove.

He pulled out a stool at the breakfast bar. 'Sit down and relax, for heaven's sake. So I answered your phone...it was no big deal.'

Caitlin sat down. 'So who else rang?' she asked, her throat tight.

'Someone called...Heidi—yes, that's it, Heidi, like the book.'

Caitlin felt herself relax slightly. At least it hadn't been David. That would have been too awkward and embarrassing.

'Heidi is also worried about you. She seems like a very lovely young woman.'

'Yes.' Caitlin nodded. 'She's my best friend.'

Ray put the plate of croissants and a cup of espresso coffee in front of her.

'So what was the message?' she asked shortly.

'They both want you to phone them.'

Caitlin nodded. It could have been worse, at least her mother didn't know the circumstances of her breakup with David. If she had started to divulge the details it would have been mortifying. And Heidi was too discreet to have said anything.

'Okay…well, thanks,' she muttered grudgingly as she took a sip of her coffee. 'But don't answer my phone again.'

Ray pulled out the chair opposite her. 'Anyone would think you were in the secret service or something.'

'I just like my privacy respected, that's all.'

Ray nodded. 'Oh, and your mother wants to come out on a visit,' he added casually.

Caitlin almost dropped the coffee in shock. 'You are joking now, aren't you?' she asked hopefully.

Ray shook his head. 'I'm afraid I had to tell her about the sorry state of your house. She was most concerned.'

'You did what?' Caitlin put the coffee-cup down in the saucer with a clatter. 'Are you joking?'

'No. She's your mother, Caitlin, she asked me directly about your circumstances, so out of respect I had to tell her.'

Caitlin's eyes darkened with fury. 'You did that on purpose, didn't you?'

'I don't know what you mean.' Ray shrugged, but there was a gleam of humour in his dark eyes that said he knew exactly what he had done.

'Yes, you do. You told my mother how bad the house was in the hope she'd talk me into selling to you. That was below the belt, Ray.'

'Rubbish.' Ray shook his head. 'But, yes, I have to admit that I hope you will see sense about keeping that place.'

'Just how badly do you want that land?' she asked suddenly.

'Not badly enough to increase my offer, if that's what you mean,' he said succinctly.

Caitlin pushed the croissants away and stood up. 'Come on, then, let's go. The sooner you take me back to the house, the sooner I can decide what I'm going to do.'

Ray sipped his coffee and made no hurry to follow. 'You haven't finished your breakfast. Your mother would be most upset.'

'Well, my mother is not here, is she?'

'Not yet.' He grinned.

The drive back to her house was totally different from the journey last night. They had the windows of the car down and the breeze that blew through her hair was warm and scented with the fragrance of the eucalyptus trees that lined the tarmac road. The sky was a dazzling blue, the landscape dotted with wild flowers and as they pulled up at the front of her house even that looked different. Yesterday it had seemed sad and dilapidated, but this morning it seemed to have gained a certain look of charm. The terracotta roof glowed in the sunshine and the peeling yellow paint on the walls seemed almost quaint surrounded by the tangle of ivy and wisteria that curved around the windows.

'It needs a lot of work and money spending on it, doesn't it?' Ray said as she climbed out of the car.

'Actually I was just thinking that it doesn't look as bad as I'd thought.' She shaded her eyes to look up at it, and then slanted him a wry look over the bonnet of the car. 'In fact, I'd go so far as to say I'm pleasantly surprised. I really like it.'

Ray shook his head. 'It's up to you what you do, of course, but let me tell you, I know for a fact it needs a new roof, plus it is probably infested with woodworm.'

'No one would ever guess you don't want me to stay here,' she said with a grin.

'I didn't say that.' He smiled back at her. 'On the contrary, I was just trying to be helpful.'

Something about the way he looked at her made her senses swim. Hastily she looked away from him. 'Sure you were.'

She walked over towards her car. The mud around the wheels had dried into solid red soil. 'So, any suggestions on how I get my car out of this rut?' she asked lightly.

He didn't answer immediately, but when she glanced over at him she saw that he was taking a long-handled shovel from the back of the car.

'You are organised.'

'Prepare for any eventuality, that is my motto,' he said and met her eyes with a cool steady look. 'You'll have to remember that if you are going to stay around here.'

She watched as he rolled up his sleeves and then started to dig beside each wheel of the car. He made the work look effortless, but in the dazzling heat of the sun she doubted it was. As his huge shoulders heaved against the hard soil Caitlin wondered idly if he worked out in order to keep such a wonderful physique. There was a raw sexuality about him that despite all her best intentions, drew her attention...fascinated her. But then it had always been like that. From the moment she had opened Murdo's front door to him, she had been disconcertingly conscious of his sex appeal.

He turned. 'Do you want to get in and start the engine now, try and drive it out?'

'Yes, certainly.' Annoyed by the thoughts that had been going through her mind, she took her keys out of her bag and unlocked the car. Okay, he was a very handsome man, she told herself, but he had danger written all over him, she wasn't interested in him. The next man she got involved with was going to be safe and dependable, a true family man. She certainly didn't want any dizzying heights—it was too far to fall.

A wall of heat hit her as she opened the car door, along with the smell of burning vinyl. Gingerly she slid into the driving seat and started the engine. It spluttered into life and on Ray's instruction she eased it forward so that it climbed easily out of its hole and back onto the solid safety of the road.

Relief flooded through her. 'Thank you so much,' she said as she got out of the vehicle, this time leaving the windows down. 'You've been very kind and I'm totally in your debt,' she added impulsively.

'That's true.' He smiled at her, a teasing light in his eyes. 'So, what are you doing on Monday night?' he asked suddenly.

Her stomach seemed to go into free fall. 'Monday?' She stared at him blankly, the question catching her completely by surprise.

'Day after tomorrow,' he informed her, leaning back against the bonnet of her car and fixing her with that nonchalant dark-eyed stare that seemed to slice straight through to her bones.

She rubbed the palms of her hands against her jeans and found they were wet with a perspiration that had little to do with heat, and her mouth felt suddenly dry with panic.

He noted the sudden vulnerable light in the beauty of her green eyes, before she looked away from him.

'Well, if you are asking me out, Ray...I'm not really ready to start dating again.' Her heart hammered fiercely against her chest. She felt like a teenager who had never been asked out before.

'Relax.' In contrast to her he sounded totally cool. 'I'm not asking you out.'

'Oh!' Her glance skated back to meet with his and she could feel her cheeks going from orange to a shade of beetroot. 'What are you asking me, then?'

He grinned. 'I'm giving a dinner party for some business clients, and I could do with someone to assist me.'

'You want me to cook for you?' She was startled by the request, and to think she had imagined he was asking her out! Embarrassment mingled with annoyance now.

Honestly, the cheek of the guy! she thought crossly.

'No, I don't want you to cook for me. I'm getting caterers in. All I really need is for you to act as hostess for the evening, just so things are kept flowing easily.'

'Oh!' She was momentarily puzzled. 'I'm not so sure about that,' she said cautiously. 'Isn't that something your girlfriend should be doing?'

'It's okay, you won't be treading on anyone's toes, I assure you,' he said with a smile, then added with a teasing gleam in his eye, 'I'm between lovers at the moment so you'd be doing me a big favour.'

'Well...' She wasn't quite sure what to say to that.

'Thanks, Caitlin.' He swept on decisively. 'Tell you what, I'll come back this afternoon to see how you are getting on here and we can make arrangements for the evening then.'

Before she had a chance to say anything else he had turned away and was heading back towards his car. She watched helplessly as he opened the boot and threw the shovel in, before driving off with a casual wave of his hand.

Caitlin shook her head and felt slightly be-mused by the speed with which she had been railroaded into that! 'Honestly!' she muttered to herself as she opened her bag to get the key of the house. As if she didn't have enough to think about.

The front door squeaked in protest as she pushed it open and peered inside. If the outside of the building had suddenly acquired a charm of its own under the blaze of the Mediterranean sun, the same could not be said about the interior. It was just as dark and just as creepy as she had thought it was yesterday. The floorboards were uneven and the staircase looked as if a few of the steps were rotted through. Maybe Ray was right about the wood-worm, she thought as she walked across the lounge area. Gingerly she felt around the case-ment of the window looking for the fastenings so that she could throw open the shutters.

When she finally found them sunlight flooded into the room, and for a moment all she could see were dust particles dancing in the air. Then slowly she took in her surround-ings. It was a good-sized room with a huge stone fireplace at one end. Hastily she flicked the dustsheets off the furniture. The blue sofa looked soft and comfortable. A large cream rug covered the centre of the room; it was covered in a grey layer of dust and had definitely seen better days. But she felt a stir of excitement inside her—the place had definite possibilities.

She walked through to the kitchen. It had a quaint old-fashioned charm, the units were dark wood and some of the doors were hanging off. But there was a large Belfast sink and what looked like an old wood-burning stove. A dining room led off to the left. But instead of walking through there, Caitlin unbolted the back door and walked outside. She found herself in a sunny courtyard with a crazy-paving path that led down through a small grove of almond and olive trees. She walked through the dappled shade down the path and as it turned a corner she found herself in a field criss-crossed with the stubbly growth of vines. Someone had tied a rope swing from an almond tree and she perched herself gingerly on the old wooden seat and looked back towards the house.

She could see that some of the red roof tiles were missing and one of the chimney pots looked as if it had a bush growing from it. The place definitely needed a lot of money spending on it, money she probably didn't have. But that didn't stop the pure burst of joy that assailed her. The house had definite potential and she loved it! Loved the red roof and the old shuttered windows, loved the blue irises that lined the path and the blossom on the almond trees. If it took every ounce of her energy and her last penny, she wanted this property.

When Ray returned it was late afternoon. The front door was open and he stood on the doorstep and called her name. There was no answer so he stepped inside. The strong odour of bleach hit him. The lounge was completely empty of furniture; the windows were open and the floors scrubbed to a deep honey yellow.

'Caitlin.' He raised his voice an octave but there was still no reply. Gingerly he made his way over the clean floor and into the kitchen. And that was where he found her. She was wearing a pair of denim shorts and a blue halter-neck top and she was on her hands and knees on the floor, scrubbing with an old wooden brush, singing tunelessly at the top of her voice as she worked. It took a moment for him to realise that she was listening to a Walkman because she had her back to him and he couldn't see the earphones. It was only as she turned slightly to rinse her brush in the bucket of water beside her that he saw the wire leading up under her dark hair and saw the blue machine clipped to the front of her belt.

She still hadn't seen him and he smiled to himself as he watched the way she was working. Her energy fascinated him, as did the wiggle of her very shapely bottom in the tight-fitting shorts.

She sang away to herself as she sat back on her heels to survey her work; stretching slightly as if her shoulders were stiff. Ray had a brief glimpse of her flat midriff and the up-tilted swell of generous breasts. And from nowhere he felt the heat of sexual attraction hit him hard.

'Caitlin.' Impatient with himself, he stepped forward into the periphery of her vision.

'Oh, gosh, you startled me!' Flustered, she

pulled the headphones off her ears. Her hair fell glossy and fluid around her shoulders as she threw it back from her face to look at him. The sound of music, tinny and contorted through the wire, sang on for a second before she clicked a button off. 'How long have you been standing there?'

'Only a few minutes. I did call you several times but you were too busy singing.' He noticed with amusement that she blushed. He liked the way he was able to make her blush; it stirred up a feeling of devilment inside him, made him want to wind her up…see the soft swell of colour increase even further.

'You could enter for the Eurovision with a voice like that,' he added softly. 'Incredible!'

'Very funny.'

He smiled as he saw the soft pink glow spread over the top of her cheekbones. He wondered if she would blush like that if he kissed her…what she would look like with her hair spread out around her on white pillows, the flush of lovemaking still on her skin.

'I see you've been down to the village.' He transferred his attention to the basket of groceries that was sitting on the sideboard.

'No, I haven't ventured as far as that. I just went into the little shop a couple of miles down the road.' She got to her feet and lifted the bucket of water to throw it away. 'I was pleasantly surprised to find that they stock most things.'

'Ah, Madeline's shop.' He nodded. 'Yes, it's very convenient.'

'She's very friendly as well and spoke perfect English. She was telling me that her nephew is a builder. She is going to send him up to see me so that he can give me an estimate on work that I want doing.'

Ray's eyebrows rose. 'From that...and all the work you are doing here, am I to deduce that you have made up your mind to stay?'

'Yes.' She answered with her back towards him as she washed her hands under the cold-water tap. A necessity as the only hot water she had had been boiled on the stove. When he made no immediate reply she turned and met his gaze. 'Look, I know you think I'm mad and I know you want the land here...but I've decided to give it my best shot,' she told him honestly. 'So I'm sorry but I will have to turn down your...generous offer to buy the place.'

He frowned. 'I think you are making a mistake.'

His words irritated her; obviously he wanted rid of her. 'Yes, well, it's my mistake to make, isn't it?'

'Certainly.' He inclined his head. 'But at least wait until after the builders have given you their estimates before closing your mind completely to my offer.'

Caitlin shook her head. 'I want the house. I'm sorry, Ray. I've made my mind up—'

'And I'd advise you to get more than one estimate on the work that needs doing here,' he cut across her as if she hadn't spoken. 'Madeline's nephew, Patrick, is a willing worker but inexperienced.'

'Yes, I know how the game works. I get a few estimates and choose the best.'

He nodded. 'And remember the best doesn't always equal the cheapest.'

She glared at him. 'You think I'm a helpless female, don't you?'

'No.' He smiled to himself as he saw her eyes blaze. 'I'm just giving you some advice.'

'No, you're not. You're thinking, She's not going to last here... I'll give her two months and then offer her less for the land and by that time she will be so broke and so ready to leave that she'll take it.'

'Maybe I am.' He laughed at the look of outrage in her eyes. 'You don't know what you are taking on here, Caitlin—'

'Well, whatever I am taking on, I'm going to give it my best shot,' she said firmly. 'So, now that we've sorted that out, shall we have a coffee and discuss Monday night?'

Ray shrugged. 'Okay. We'll put the subject of you selling in abeyance. And we'll discuss it again when you've had the builders' reports.'

Caitlin ignored that. She didn't want to discuss the subject again, she desperately wanted to stay here and make it work. 'So what time do you want me to come over on Monday night?' she asked lightly instead as she filled a pan of water to put on the stove.

'About six-thirty, but don't worry, I'll call for you. Whereabouts will you be staying? There's a hotel in the village that's very good—'

'Hotel?' Caitlin frowned and looked over at him. 'Why would I stay in a hotel? I'm staying here.'

'You are not thinking of sleeping here to-night, are you?' He sounded shocked.

'Of course I am. This is going to be my home now.' She glanced around at him. 'Will dried milk do? As I have no fridge yet I didn't bother buying fresh.'

'I take my coffee black. But, Caitlin, you can't possibly stay in this house.' His dark eyes seemed to pierce right into hers with steady determination.

'Why not?'

'Well, for one thing, it's got no electricity.'

'I've already sorted that problem.' She reached into her shopping and held up a candle. 'I've been told it won't be possible to re-connect me for a few weeks. So unless I want to wander around in pitch-black these will suffice.'

He shook his head. 'I can't see how you can possibly contemplate sleeping here until you have a new staircase and a new roof.'

'I'm going to sleep downstairs in the dining room.' She took some mugs from a box. 'I'm afraid you'll have to have instant coffee. It will be a while before things start to get civilised around here.'

'You're not kidding.' Ray's voice was derisive. 'Look, you'd better stay with me up at the house, at least until you've got the electricity fixed.'

'That's a very kind offer, Ray, but honestly I'll be fine.'

'I don't think so.' He reached out and touched her lightly on the face. 'Come and stay with me, Caitlin, for a few days at least. I don't like to think of you here alone.'

The gentleness of his tone, the touch of his hand and the thought of spending even more time with him sent a mixture of panic and pleasure through her in wildly disconcerting waves.

The water in the pan started to bubble. A bit like her temperature around him, she thought wryly as she stepped back from him. 'That's very kind of you, Ray. But this place isn't as bad as you think.'

That statement met with silence. Hastily she turned away from him and made the coffee.

'Actually I made a great discovery as I was moving the furniture from the lounge. The sofa pulls out into a bed. So I'll be fine on that.'

There was a lot of incredulity on his face as she handed him his drink. 'The place is uninhabitable,' he said bluntly.

'No, it's not. I've got this great old stove.' She patted the bar on the cooker behind her. 'You can burn anything in it, and I found a load of old wood out the back so it should keep me going for ages.'

He still didn't look convinced so she put down her coffee. 'Downstairs is fine, Ray, and there is even a downstairs bathroom. Come on, I'll show you what I've done to the back room this morning.'

Ray followed her through a door at the far end of the kitchen into the dining room. It was a charming space with south-facing windows that looked out towards the olive grove and the purple mountains beyond. Like the other downstairs rooms, she had obviously scrubbed it out. There was a white tablecloth on the pine dining table and a white jug of blue irises. The sofa bed was under the window and was already made up with white linen, a colourful patchwork quilt and several scatter cushions. He had to admit that with a few womanly touches Caitlin had succeeded in making the place look comfortable and homely. Ray was impressed at what she had accomplished in such a short space of time and he felt he might have underestimated her; there seemed to be more to Caitlin than first met the eye.

'You see, this will be quite adequate for now,' she said defensively, then as she caught him looking up at the cracks in the ceiling added quickly, 'Obviously it still needs sorting out properly, but that will have to wait.'

Ray perched himself down on the arm of the sofa. 'I'll agree you've certainly made the place look a lot better.'

'I can sense the word ''however'' hovering on your lips,' she said wryly.

'Can you?' He looked over at her then and smiled. 'Maybe it is, but I won't say it...not just yet anyway. You are a very stubborn woman, Caitlin.'

She shrugged. There was a certain way he had of looking at her sometimes that made her feel almost light-headed. And she liked the way he said her name; it rolled from his tongue sometimes almost like a caress.

She tried to blot those thoughts out very firmly. Her name sounded attractive on his lips because of his accent. And he probably bestowed that look of teasing, sensual approval on a lot of women.

'So all I'll say instead is that if you have any problems you can phone me.' She watched as he put his coffee down on the window ledge and took a gold pen from the top pocket of his shirt. 'Have you got a piece of paper? I'll write down my mobile number for you.'

'I won't need to phone you, Ray,' she said determinedly, 'because I'm not going to have any problems; I've got everything under control.'

'I'm sure you have.' He grinned. 'But you never know, you might want to phone me anyway.' He reached out and caught hold of her hand. 'It doesn't matter about paper, this will do.'

She watched as he turned her wrist and proceeded to put his number on her arm in blue ink.

The touch of his hand and the cool firmness of the pen against her skin were unsettling. 'There, you can write it down somewhere safe later.' He smiled into her eyes and that was even more disquieting.

'Thanks.' Her heart was thumping against her chest in a most peculiar way. She pulled her hand away from his sharply and hastily took a step backwards. 'But as I said before I have everything under control, so you won't be getting any damsel-in-distress calls from me.'

'Well, maybe you'll change your mind and want me to rescue you when the old timbers begin to creak and the bullfrogs start their nightly chorus, or when you've had enough of playing house and waiting for builders.' He put the pen away and stood up.

'In your dreams,' she replied, her voice hardening. 'It will take more than a few frogs to make me run scared.' Now she wanted to scrub the number off her arm immediately. 'I will manage here,' she said quickly. 'Being alone doesn't bother me and, anyway, I'm expecting to have this place up and running as a bed and breakfast business by the end of the

year. There are five good-sized bedrooms upstairs that will lend themselves very nicely to
having *en suites* put in.'

'It's an ambitious project.'

'Maybe, but once I make my mind up to do
something I usually see it through to comple-
tion.' She raised her chin slightly.

'That's something else we have in common,
then.' Ray smiled and stood up. 'Well, you've
got courage, Caitlin, I'll give you that.'

There it was again, that rolling, sexy emphasis on her name. No man had a right to
sound that good as well as look that attractive.
He should come with a health warning, she
thought hazily. *Warning: this man could seriously affect your heartbeat.*

'So, anyway, I'll see you Monday night,'
she said, hastily gathering her senses.

'Yes, I'll pick you up at six-thirty,' he said,
heading towards the door.

'There's no need, I'll make my own way
over,' she told him firmly as she followed him
back through the house. Somehow it seemed
important that she arrived under her own
steam, maintained her complete independence.

She thought he was going to argue the point, but he didn't. 'Okay.' He stopped at the front doorway and looked back at her. 'And don't forget, ring if you need anything,' he said over his shoulder as he strode away towards his car.

She watched as he drove away, his vehicle crunching over the uneven surface of her drive. Then as he disappeared silence fell and darkness started to steal over the landscape.

Caitlin looked down at the number written so boldly on her arm and went inside to wash it off. But before she did, she found herself writing it down in her address book; why, she didn't know. She'd never ring him, she told herself sternly. *Never.* Then she returned her phone calls from that morning and tried to reassure her mother that she was fine.

As soon as Ray reached the château he headed for the phone and dialled his business partner in Paris. 'We've got more of a problem with plot twenty-seven than I had first thought. Yes, Murdo's property. One very determined lady is in residence and it looks like it's going to hold back the whole development.'

He tapped his fingers impatiently against the rosewood counter as he waited for the reply, and then grinned. 'Yes, she is, actually. No, I'll take care of it. It's a temporary hitch, I'm sure. Oh…and see if you can get hold of a copy of Murdo McCray's last will and testament.'

CHAPTER FOUR

CAITLIN had never lived alone before. At eighteen she had got a job at a central London hospital and had moved straight from living at home into the nurses' accommodation there. She had shared a room with two other girls and it had been a very lively time. When they hadn't been studying for exams or working they had been out partying. There had never been a dull moment...or a quiet one.

That was when she had met Julian Darcy, a first year intern, incredible-looking, and as sexy as hell. She had fallen completely under his spell. For a full year they had dated and Caitlin had honestly thought he was the one...but unfortunately Caitlin hadn't been the only one the suave doctor had been whispering sweet nothings to.

Julian was the reason she had moved away from her job in London to work in Manchester. She had moved into a flat up there with her best friend, Heidi, who was also a nurse. And slowly she had recovered her confidence and her heart. The two of them had really enjoyed sharing a flat. And again there had rarely been a time when Caitlin had felt alone. They had made lots of friends and gone out on lots of dates and then they had both fallen in love, Heidi with Peter, Caitlin with David. It had been during the run up to Heidi's wedding that David had asked her to move in with him. She hadn't said yes straight away; she hadn't been sure if it was the right thing for her. But David had been persistent. He had wooed her with bouquets of flowers, extravagant gifts. And he had told her over and over again how much he loved her, how much he needed her…and how he wanted to be with her forever.

It was the forever bit that had finally won her around. Caitlin had witnessed her own parents' divorce when she was twelve, and she never wanted to go through anything like that. Commitment was important to her. So when she had moved her things in with David's she had honestly thought it was for the rest of her life.

They had got engaged a few months later and had intended to get married the following spring but somehow the date hadn't been set for another two years.

Murdo had sometimes remarked that David wasn't her soul mate, because if he were she wouldn't have kept putting off the wedding date.

She had dismissed the notion out of hand. Now she wondered if it was true. Maybe subconsciously she had known David wasn't right for her. Maybe she had even been on the rebound from Julian?

Lying alone on the sofa bed, in the darkness and deepest silence of the French night, Caitlin reflected on the past and tried to make sense of it. Maybe she was just destined to always fall for the wrong kind of man. She'd read articles about that—about women who kept making the same kind of mistakes. Trouble was, she had tried to play safe with David…had thought he was steady and reliable…

But when she had found out about his gambling debts all her trust in him had evaporated overnight. If he had lied to her about that, what else had he lied about? And worst of all David had refused to acknowledge that he had a problem. Suddenly their life together had seemed like a façade and she just hadn't been able to go through with the commitment of marriage. After deep contemplation in the weeks that had followed, Caitlin had contacted everyone to tell them the wedding was cancelled. It was the hardest thing she had ever had to do.

At first light of dawn Caitlin got up. Work was the best way of keeping her mind off her problems. And it wasn't hard to keep busy. There was so much to do. Sunday passed in a haze of hard exertion, and then on Monday morning Patrick arrived.

He was a good-looking man in his late twenties with tousled dark hair and serious eyes. He wandered around her house with a worried look on his face, scratching his head, making Caitlin feel as if she were waiting for a life and death doctor's report.

'So what do you think, Patrick?' she asked finally when she couldn't stand the suspense of waiting any longer.

'I think,' he said in careful pidgin English, 'that the house needs much work. First it needs to be rewired...next it needs damp proof...and new stairs...new roof...'

'So how much money are we talking here? Don't forget I want new bathrooms.'

Patrick scratched his head again. 'The roof is a job for my brother Raul. But I can do everything else. It will probably take a few months. If you like you can pay me by the week and buy the materials separately.'

'That sounds acceptable... So how much do you estimate it will cost?'

Patrick named a sum that was just within her budget and a wave of relief rushed through her. However, the feeling was short-lived because it was then that Patrick delivered his bombshell.

'Unfortunately, that is not the end of the work that needs to be done,' he said slowly. 'You see, you are not connected to the main water supply here and that is something you should rectify.'

'But I've got water,' Caitlin said with a frown.

'That supply comes from a nearby well. You don't know how long it will last. Maybe a month...maybe six months...maybe six years...' Patrick shrugged. 'It is—how you say?—unreliable. You need to get connected to the mains.'

'And how much will that cost?'

'It's a big job, not one I can do,' Patrick said firmly. 'There is a lot of land here needing brand-new pipes. My cousin had a similar problem last year.'

'And how much did he pay to rectify the situation?'

Patrick shrugged and then went on to name a sum of money that, on top of all the other work that needed doing, sent her budget wildly in excess of anything she could afford.

As the sun started to fade and Caitlin got ready for her evening with Ray, she was still reeling from Patrick's assessment. If the water ran out she would be beaten here before she had even started. But if she fixed the water first she wouldn't be able to afford the structural work on the house. It was a catch-22 situation and a depressing thought. However, as she washed her hair in cold water and boiled pans of water in order to have the shallowest of baths she tried to convince herself that every-thing would be okay. Maybe the water would last six years. After all that rain the other day maybe sixteen years! Patrick wasn't an expert on the subject; he had admitted that, so she would look on the bright side.

Trying to forget about her financial problems, Caitlin stepped into her black dress and peered at her reflection in the small vanity mirror. The last time she had worn this dress had been to a cocktail party for David's work. Back then it had been a snug fit over her hips; now it seemed to hang a little loose. However, in the soft glow of candlelight she looked presentable. The cold water seemed to have given her hair a luxuriant shine and her skin had a soft honey glow from two days of sunshine. But would she pass scrutiny under the blaze of electric light at Ray's residence? Caitlin felt a flutter of butterflies. Then, annoyed with herself, she stepped away from the mirror and picked up her bag. It didn't matter what she looked like; she wasn't trying to impress Ray, and this wasn't a date.

As she blew out the candles in the dining room and walked through to the lounge she heard a car drawing up outside. The sound was abnormally loud in the soft stillness of the night.

She peeped cautiously out from the front windows. Caitlin loved the solitude here during the days, but at night when darkness fell she had to admit to feeling a little nervous. A car door slammed and there was the sound of footsteps. Caitlin could see the dark silhouette of a man. Moonlight slanted over him, throwing a long shadow that made him appear exceptionally tall. It wasn't until he reached the top of the garden and looked up that she could see it was Ray. He was wearing a dark suit and his hair gleamed almost blue-black in the silver moonlight. Relieved that it was someone she knew, she went to open the door, swinging it wide before he had a chance to knock.

'Hi,' she said lightly. Now that she had discovered it wasn't a mad axe murderer who was making his way to her door, her heart rate should have decreased, but instead it seemed to increase wildly as her eyes connected with his. 'I thought we'd agreed that you wouldn't call for me.'

'I know.' He smiled. 'But I was passing anyway. So I thought if you were ready you might like a lift.'

'Thanks. Yes, I am ready, actually; you couldn't have timed it better. I'll just blow the candles out in here, won't be a moment.'

He stepped inside the door to wait for her and as she crossed towards the sideboard she was very conscious of the way his eyes followed her.

'You look very beautiful tonight, Caitlin,' he said softly.

'Thank you.' Her heart rocketed unsteadily, as if it were trying to escape. It was crazy to feel this nervous she told herself as she bent to extinguish the white church candles. He was just being polite; the fact that the compliment sounded dangerously provocative was just because his accent was so deliciously sexy.

'So how are things going with the house?' he asked as she made her way back towards him in darkness.

'Everything is going very well.' She made herself sound positive and upbeat; she wasn't going to admit she had problems already. 'Patrick is going to start work tomorrow.'

'I thought you were going to get a few quotes before you decided who to give the job to?'

'Yes, but I liked Patrick and he can start immediately, which is great. Time is money, after all, and the sooner I can get this place up and running, the sooner I will be recouping my expenses.'

'Sounds sensible.'

'Yes, I thought so.' Her instincts told her Patrick was a decent guy. The job would be fine. 'So how are the arrangements for dinner going?' she asked, swiftly moving on before Ray could throw any doubts on the situation.

'Everything is under control.'

Caitlin had the feeling that everything was always under control in Ray's life. He had that air of power about him.

He took hold of her arm as they walked outside. She could smell the tang of his after-shave; it was fresh and warm and immensely attractive. The touch of his fingers against the bare skin on her arm sent shooting little shivers of awareness rushing through her. It was extremely perturbing.

He opened the passenger door of his car and saw her safely inside before going around to the driver's side.

'So the catering staff have arrived, I take it?' she asked, trying to concentrate her thoughts back on the evening ahead.

Ray started the car engine. 'Yes, there was a delightful aroma of fresh herbs and roast lamb wafting through the house when I left. So you can rest assured your cooking skills will not be needed.'

'Just as well,' Caitlin said lightly. 'I had a weird dream last night that I burnt all the food for your dinner party and everyone shook their heads and said they had expected as much from *la cuisine anglaise.*'

Ray laughed at that. 'I don't know why you dreamt that. I did tell you I was getting staff in.'

'I know.' Caitlin shook her head and looked out at the dark blur of the passing landscape. She didn't tell him that in the dream Murdo had turned up at the table and demanded to know why they hadn't set their wedding date yet.

'I have been having the strangest dreams recently,' she murmured quietly.

'I'd have thought any nightmares you would have would be centred on that house of yours,' Ray said lightly.

Caitlin frowned. 'The house will be fine, Ray. It's got loads of potential.'

'Yes and loads of drawbacks.' Ray flicked her an amused glance. 'Did Patrick tell you about the water problem?'

'You know about that?' She looked over at him in surprise.

'Of course I know about it. I kept telling Murdo that it needed sorting out.'

'Well, it's obviously been like that for years, so I don't see any reason to rush into fixing it just yet.'

'You must be joking. If you want my advice that's the first job you should do.'

'Yes, well, I've got Patrick's advice, thank you, and that's all I need at the moment.'

'He won't be able to fix the water problem, you'll have to get other contractors in for that, and in my opinion you should budget at least double what Patrick has told you it will cost.'

'Double?' Caitlin felt her heart bounce somewhere down into her shoes. 'That's crazy.

With respect, Ray, I don't think you know what you are talking about.'

'I know that place is a money pit.' Ray shrugged.

'Maybe, but I've got my budget well planned out.' Caitlin angled her chin upwards defiantly. Ray's know-it-all attitude really was starting to irritate.

Ray glanced over at her and smiled to himself. 'So how much is your budget for the place?'

'That's really none of your business,' she muttered.

'Well, let's see…let me guess.' Ray pursed his lips thoughtfully, before naming the exact sum that she had discussed with Patrick.

Caitlin turned to look at him in astonishment. 'How on earth do you know that?'

He smiled. 'I've been in Madeline's shop,' he said pointedly. 'Patrick is Madeline's nephew.'

'Yes, I know that, but it doesn't give her the right to discuss my business.' Caitlin was furious.

Ray pulled the car to a standstill outside the château. Then he turned to look at her. 'She's just a concerned neighbour, Caitlin. The fact is that Murdo had that work priced years ago and it was twice the sum you are bandying about with Patrick now.'

'Well, maybe I'm more resourceful than Murdo.' Caitlin reached for the car handle. 'And I'm not going to worry about water because, let's face it, after that storm the other night water levels must be high.'

'This is early spring, Caitlin,' Ray said quietly.

'Ray, if you don't mind I don't want to discuss this a moment longer,' Caitlin said as she got out of the car.

Ray shook his head. He had to admit he liked her determination. It was almost a pity that she was going to fail.

There was an air of quiet sophistication about the house. The dining room looked resplendent, the polished table was laid with sparkling silver and cut-glass crystal and there were three members of staff in the kitchen who were going to serve the meal.

As Ray talked to the chef about the menu Caitlin tried not to dwell on their conversation in the car. She knew what Ray's game was.

He wanted her land; it was in his interest to put her off staying here. Angrily she repositioned a vase of freshly cut dark red roses so that it didn't obscure anyone's view on the table. But apart from that there was nothing for her to do.

'I don't think you really needed me here tonight at all, Ray,' she said as the chef departed.

Ray didn't answer her immediately and she turned to find him leaning against the doorframe, watching her with a lazy, almost indolent stare.

'Now, you are not going to sulk all evening just because I'm right about your house, are you, *chéri?*' he asked softly, almost teasingly.

'You're not right about the house,' she retorted crisply. 'And I never sulk.'

He smiled at that. 'Good. Then how about a pre-dinner drink?' He moved to the sideboard.

'A glass of white wine would be nice,' she said.

Their hands touched briefly as she took the glass. 'Thanks.' She took a step backwards and searched for something to say to fill the silence that suddenly seemed to have opened between them.

She could feel his eyes moving over her in an assessing manner, as if he was taking in every detail about her dress and her hair.

'And in answer to your earlier question I really do appreciate you being here tonight,' he said softly.

She looked up and met the directness of his eyes and for some reason her heart seemed to give a nervous thud of anticipation. He looked extremely handsome in the dark suit, the pristine whiteness of his shirt throwing his olive skin and dark hair into sharp contrast. But there was also an air of danger about him, she thought warily. She couldn't explain it, but there was something about him that made her feel infinitely nervous. Maybe it was the predatory way he looked at her sometimes...or the sensual curve of his lips. Or that way he had of cutting straight through her defences just with his eyes, making her feel as if he could see straight into her soul.

'So...who is coming, this evening?' she asked briskly, trying to dismiss that notion.

'My business partner Philippe and his wife Sadie. Philippe runs our office in Paris so it's a chance for us to touch base. Also a new business client, Roger Delaware, with his partner Sharon, who I am hoping will put a lot of work our way over the next few months.'

'Sounds like quite an important evening for you.'

'Yes...I must admit I would like Roger to sign up with us. He's planning to build a new hotel in Cannes. It's just the type of development our company likes. So I'm hoping tonight will help swing things in our favour.'

'So the evening is more about business than pleasure.'

'Well, I'm hoping it's going to be about both.'

His dark eyes held with hers for a moment and then hastily she looked away before she could be sucked towards that magnetic, charismatic appeal. If captivating the opposite sex was an art form, Ray had the talent in spades, she thought warily. It seemed almost to come naturally to him. She wondered how many women had been passionately in love with him, only to have their hearts broken...probably hundreds. It would be a brave woman who took Ray on. 'So who usually acts as your hostess on these occasions?' she asked curiously, trying to concentrate on the golden liquid in her glass rather than on him.

'For the last few months a woman called Claudette. But things didn't work out between us.' He shrugged in that Gallic way of his. 'That's life.'

He didn't sound too upset, which led Caitlin to suspect that he'd been the one to finish it. 'You strike me as the kind of man who probably breaks a lot of hearts.' She spoke impulsively.

'Do I?' He looked amused. 'Why's that?'

'I don't know.' Her eyes moved over him contemplatively. 'Something about you.'

'Well, I enjoy the company of women and I am a red-blooded male, but I hope I don't break hearts. It certainly is not my intention— in fact I'm very careful about the women I choose to have relationships with. And I am always honest and up front about the fact that I have no wish to get married again.'

'You loved your wife very much, didn't you?' Caitlin reflected. She watched the way his eyes seemed to darken with some emotion she couldn't begin to analyse. 'Murdo told me,' she murmured hastily. 'And I'm sorry, I didn't mean to pry.'

'That's okay. You're right, I did love my wife...very much.'

Caitlin looked away from him, feeling sorry that she had intruded on something so intensely personal.

'So what about you? Do you break hearts, Caitlin?' he asked, changing the subject with that swift ease that never failed to disconcert her.

'I hope not.'

'But it must have been you who called the wedding off—no man in his right mind would have done that.'

'Thanks for the vote of confidence,' she said wryly, a little suspicious of the flattery. She hesitated. 'I did call it off...but it wasn't something I wanted to do...'

'You did it because you had no choice, because he hurt you.' It was a statement rather than a question, so she made no reply.

'You know, the best way to get over one man is to get involved with another.' He put a

hand under her chin and tipped her face upwards so that she was forced to look at him
again. 'Having a little fun helps clear the mind
and heal the heart.'

The gentle touch of his hand against her skin
seemed to burn like a branding iron. She really
tried not to blush, but she could feel her skin
heating up as if someone had lit a fire under
her.

'Is that what you do?' She stepped back,
trying to break the intimate spell that suddenly
seemed to be swirling powerfully between
them. 'Jump straight from one relationship into
another?'

'I haven't got a broken heart,' he said
lightly.

'I see.' She took a sip of her wine and gathered herself together. 'I'm afraid, Ray, that
I've got some bad news for you.' She forced
a lightly teasing note into her voice and met
his eyes directly.

'Apart from not selling me your property,
you mean?' He smiled.

'Oh, yes, apart from that.' She waved a hand
in airy dismissal and angled her head to one
side. 'The thing is, Ray...and brace yourself

for this…the thing is that you are never going to make an agony aunt. Your advice is rubbish.'

He looked at her and his lips curved in a smile that also lit his eyes. Then he laughed, a warm, genuine laugh that somehow also seemed to set her pulses racing. 'I like you, Caitlin,' he said with a shake of his head. 'I have to tell you I like you very much…'

Their eyes met and for a moment she was tempted to say she liked him too. But it was a fleeting thought and one she immediately buried.

To her relief the shrill ring of the front doorbell interrupted them. 'That will probably be Philippe and Sadie.' Ray turned away. 'They said they would be early.'

Ray's business partner and his wife were both French. Philippe was about forty-five, slightly on the portly side, his dark hair greying at the temples. He had an air of sophistication; here was a shrewd man who was successful in business and very laid back about it. His wife Sadie was about ten years younger than him and stunning. Her dark hair was coiled into an attractive style high on her head, emphasising her delicate features, her high cheekbones and dark almond-shaped eyes. Her cream dress was obviously from a designer boutique in Paris, but even if it had been from a charity shop she would have looked good in it, because her figure was superb, voluptuous yet slender. She possessed the kind of chic style that seemed to come so naturally to continental women.

'It's lovely to meet you, Caitlin,' she said as she kissed the air at either side of Caitlin's cheeks. 'I've heard all about you.'

'Have you?' Caitlin looked over at Ray in surprise and he smiled. 'Oh, yes, I've told Philippe and Sadie all about my pesky neighbour who stubbornly refuses to sell out to me.'

'Are you still going on about that land, *chéri?*' Sadie stood on tiptoe to kiss Ray. Caitlin noticed that her scarlet lips made contact with Ray's skin, and her hands lingered on his arms as she drew back to look up at him playfully. 'Honestly, you own most of the countryside around here as it is.'

Caitlin noticed that Philippe sent her a warning look, as if she was being too outspoken, but Sadie seemed unconcerned. And so did Ray.

'I do,' he replied easily, a gleam in his eye. 'But that doesn't stop me wanting more. However, I've discovered my new neighbour has other assets so I'm content to leave things as they are...for now.'

'What do you mean, ''other assets''?' Caitlin asked distractedly, unsure if she liked the direction of this conversation.

Ray gave her that lopsided grin that she was starting to recognise. 'I mean the pleasure of your company, of course.'

Caitlin shook her head. She wasn't going to allow herself to be affected by Ray's compliments. When the mood struck him he probably knew all the right things to say to make a woman feel special and get what he wanted. And of course he was a born flirt. She remembered the way he'd looked at her earlier. *You know, the best way to get over one man is to get involved with another...* He'd been teasing her, of course, and it didn't necessarily mean a thing, but if she were to let down her guard and take him seriously she'd be courting trouble.

Instead she turned her attention to Sadie as they moved into the lounge.

'Have you come all the way down from Paris for dinner tonight?'

Sadie smiled. 'Yes, we flew down to Nice and motored up. We often do that, and of course we have a potential new client joining us tonight so it's pretty important to secure that contract.'

'Let's hope his partner, Sharon, is in a better mood tonight than the last time we got together.' Philippe sighed. 'Good job you're here, Caitlin, otherwise we might never get this contract.'

'Why is that?' Caitlin asked in puzzlement.

'You mean Ray hasn't told you?' Sadie laughed. 'I'm afraid Sharon has a bad case of lust for Ray. It was quite embarrassing last time we got together. And we were worried it would make Roger back out of doing business with us altogether.'

'Oh, I see.' Caitlin smiled over at Ray. 'So much for the pleasure of my company.'

'I told you, Caitlin, you are quite an asset,' he said without a shade of remorse. Then he smiled that warm smile that seemed to light up his eyes.

The doorbell rang and Ray got up to answer it.

'He's incorrigible, isn't he?' Sadie laughed. 'And gorgeous—everyone falls in love with him. I have lost count of the beautiful women that have been on his arm. Is that not so, Philippe?'

'He just hasn't found the right person yet,' Philippe said, somewhat crossly. 'I don't think you should be giving Caitlin the wrong idea.'

Caitlin wanted to say that she didn't care and that she wasn't one of his many girl-friends, but she didn't get the chance because Ray entered the room with his remaining guests.

As the evening progressed Caitlin relaxed. Ray's friends were all very agreeable and he was certainly a charming and attentive host. She watched him surreptitiously during dinner and noted how the women hung on his every word. She also saw exactly what Sadie meant about the partner of their new business client. Sharon was definitely smitten by Ray. The woman was in her mid thirties, a rather glam-

orous blonde with a shapely figure and smoul-
dering blue eyes. As the wine flowed she became more and more outrageously flirtatious,
fluttering her eyelashes at Ray and making bla-
tant references as to how attractive she found
him.

Ray handled the situation with suave ease
and Roger Delaware didn't look too perturbed
by his partner's behaviour, but Caitlin agreed
with Sadie: businesswise the situation did not
bode well.

'So what do you do for a living, Caitlin?'
Roger Delaware asked suddenly as Sharon
reached across the table to place a hand on
Ray's in order to tell him how wonderful dinner had been.

Caitlin couldn't help feeling sorry for Roger.
He seemed a pleasant guy, a lot older than
Sharon—he could possibly have been in his
early sixties—but very attractive.

'I have a small holding not far from here
and I'm converting it into a bed and breakfast
business,' she answered lightly.

'Really. How interesting. That's how I made
my money, you know, in the hotel business
back in the USA. Started in Texas and grad-

ually worked my way through each state. Now I'm moving my attention to the continent. I'm hoping Ray is going to design a fine building for me.'

'I'm sure he will, I've heard Ray is very talented,' Caitlin said with a wry smile. She had often listened as Murdo had waxed lyrical about Ray's skill as an architect.

'Yes, he has an unrivalled reputation, I know that.' Roger nodded. 'But it comes at a price...' He shook his head.

'Roger, if you started out in Texas I'm sure you know that only the ropey ends of the meat trade are cheap, you have to pay prime money for prime steak.'

Roger laughed at that heartily. 'You've got a point, Caitlin, you've got a point.'

'Well, I don't know too much about Ray's business dealings,' Caitlin admitted, 'but I *do* know he's very much in demand. Anybody who is anybody wants Ray Pascal. I suppose it's like buying a Prada handbag or Jimmy Choo shoes—there is a certain chic about having them.'

'You think so...?' Roger nodded. 'Yes, I suppose you are right, and I have a certain image to maintain. My hotels are known for their style.'

Caitlin smiled back at him and reached to top up his wineglass.

'So tell me about your B&B.' Roger leaned a little closer.

'Well, it's small and I'm certainly not going to make a fortune out of it. But it will suit me. After years of living in cities it's nice to be out here in the fresh air of the countryside. And renovating the place is proving to be quite a challenge.'

'A challenge is putting it mildly,' Ray interjected as he removed his hand from under Sharon's for the second time. 'I think Caitlin must have the courage of a lion to take the place on.'

'I'm enjoying it.' Caitlin shrugged. 'But I have a lot to learn. There is a small vineyard that I would like to get up and running, and an olive grove that I'm sure I could make extra money out of. Only problem is my knowledge is pretty limited.'

'Are you living in Murdo's old place?' Philippe asked suddenly.

Caitlin nodded.

'Well, it's structurally unsound, isn't it?' Philippe glanced over towards Ray for clarification. 'Didn't you have surveyors go to look at it one time for Murdo?'

'I don't remember that, Philippe,' Ray said with an edge of impatience in his tone.

Caitlin wondered if it was her imagination, but she thought Philippe looked annoyed by Ray's reply.

'But I know if Caitlin doesn't get connected to the water mains she might be out of water there some time soon,' Ray continued with a shrug.

Caitlin fidgeted in her chair. She didn't want to talk about this. 'The place is fine; it just needs a bit of time and some TLC.'

'So how long have you and Ray been an item?' Sharon suddenly cut across all the talk of Caitlin's house, her tone bored. Then she fixed Caitlin with a direct look that was so forceful it was almost aggressive.

Suddenly Caitlin was conscious of everyone's eyes on her. She wanted to say categorically that she and Ray were not dating...but she knew very well Ray was hoping her presence here as his partner would encourage

Roger to do business with them. So she didn't know how to answer. 'Well…I…'

Ray came to her rescue. 'Caitlin and I met last year through a mutual friend of ours. But it's only in the last few weeks that romance has blossomed, is that not so, *chéri?*' He leaned across and squeezed her hand gently as he spoke.

She met the challenging light in his dark eyes and knew very well that he was giving her the standpoint from which to back him up. 'Eh…yes. It's been an unexpected development…' She went along with him hesitantly and he smiled.

'Totally out of the blue,' he agreed. 'But that's the thing about the love bug—you never know when it will bite. I went over to Caitlin's one day and there she was singing away to herself looking extremely fetching and I just thought…she's perfect…the most beautiful woman I have ever seen…'

Caitlin pulled her hand away from his uncomfortably. He was going over the top now. 'Don't exaggerate, *darling,*' she warned him crisply.

His smile widened as if he found her embarrassment endearing.

'Let's move into the lounge and have coffee, shall we?' Caitlin pushed her chair back from the table, wanting to put an end to this very quickly.

'Good idea,' Ray agreed easily. 'Then maybe we can talk a little business, Roger.'

'Certainly.' Roger's tone was jovial. 'We will have to get things moving pretty quickly with this project, Ray. Pull out all the stops.'

Caitlin excused herself and headed for the kitchen. The catering staff had left over an hour ago but the place was spotless. She busied herself putting cups and saucers on a tray as she waited for the water to boil.

Ray followed her into the room a few minutes later.

'So which am I?' he inquired with a grin. 'The prime piece of meat or the designer accessory?'

She swung a glance around at him, humour dancing in her green eyes. 'Sorry, was I a bit over the top?'

'Hey, I'm not complaining. Whatever you've said to him it seems to have worked.

He's no longer haggling over the price, it's when can I start.'

'I think that's probably down to the very impressive meal,' Caitlin said dismissively.

'And maybe the way you smiled at him,' Ray added softly.

She looked over at him.

'Thanks for helping me out in there.' Something about the way he said that, the way he met her eyes, sent little darts of awareness pulsating through her.

'That's okay.' She shrugged the feeling away and then laughed. 'You dug me out of a hole and I dug you out of one. We'll call it even shall we?'

'If you want.' He crossed to stand beside her.

'Did you really send a surveyor up to Murdo's property once?' She tried to concentrate on the conversation and not on the way he was watching her, with that intense, steady gaze.

'No, Philippe must have been confusing your house with somewhere else.'

'Thank heavens for that.' She gave a wry smile. 'At least the place isn't going to fall down before I can fix it.'

'No, it's not going to fall down.' He smiled and tucked a strand of her hair behind her ear so that he could see her face more clearly. 'You hide behind your hair sometimes, do you know that?'

'Do I?' Her voice wavered a little; the touch of his hand had sent volts of electricity through her like lightning through a conductor.

Desperately she searched for something to say…something that was light and distracting. 'Sharon was rather persistent, I thought.'

'Very, but you played the part of girlfriend perfectly. In fact, is there no end to your talents?' He lowered his voice provocatively.

He stepped even closer. She could smell the evocative tang of his aftershave; feel the heat of his body just a whisper away from hers.

As she tried to move away from him he put a detaining hand on her arm and then somehow she found herself facing him, looking up at him instead.

She noticed how his eyes were on her lips and her heart started to thump out of control.

'I suppose you should get back to your guests...' She made an attempt at sounding sensible but her voice had an unsteady, husky quality.

'Ray...?' It was Sharon's voice calling him from the hall, but neither of them moved. It was as if they were locked in their own private world.

'Ray, where are you?'

The voice came nearer.

'I think your prospective mistress is looking for you...' Caitlin tried to force her brain into some semblance of sanity.

'Not funny, Caitlin,' Ray admonished. He reached up and brushed his fingers softly over her high cheekbones, following the contours of her face gently down to the sensitive area at the side of her neck. The caress sent thrilling little shivers of sensation shooting through her. 'And, anyway, I've got someone else in mind for that position.'

Before she could even formulate a reply his head lowered closer to hers; she could feel the softness of his breath against her skin, see the flecks of deepest gold in his dark eyes.

'Ray...' Her breath came out in a rush as she whispered his name. He covered her lips with the warmth of his, then gently... slowly...tasted her, caressed her with lips that were dominantly masterful...yet tenderly possessive. The sensation was one of overwhelming eroticism; it was as if he were pulling every string of her consciousness, tugging deep inside her to find the sensual core of her womanhood.

Caitlin couldn't help herself responding. She moved her hands to rest against his shoulder, feeling his strength beneath her fingers as they curved into his shirt. Her lips trembled with need against his. Somehow reality faded away and all she was left with was a sense of need...an almost desperate hunger that was like a gnawing ache. She heard herself give a small, breathless whimper as he moved even closer, crushing her body against his.

She could feel the warmth of his chest burning through to the softness of her breast, and the sensation made her tingle with pleasure. She wanted to be closer... She wanted to immerse herself in him, feel the pleasure of his hands against her naked skin.

'Sorry to interrupt.' Sharon's cool voice from the doorway made them break apart.

'Sorry, Sharon, we didn't hear you come in.' Ray sounded remarkably offhand. But Caitlin's emotions were raging all over the place. She felt mortified at how she had responded to him, and at the same time she was angry with Sharon for interrupting, because she wanted so much more...

'I did call a couple of times.' Sharon's eyes held Caitlin's; there was venom in their blue depths. 'But you obviously had other things on your mind.'

'Yes, we did.' Ray sounded completely unconcerned. 'So, what can we do for you, Sharon?'

'Claudette is on the phone for you,' Sharon answered pointedly.

'Okay, I'm coming.' Ray flicked a glance at Caitlin and smiled as he saw the glow of heat high on her cheekbones, the overbright sparkle in her green eyes. 'I'll leave you to finish the coffee uninterrupted, Caitlin.'

'Good idea.' She turned away from him and reached for the kettle.

Her hand shook a little as she poured boiling water into the coffee pot. She was annoyed with herself for feeling so shook up. Ray had kissed her because flirting and seduction were just a game to him, and the fact Sharon was around to witness their closeness was a bonus. She should shrug the moment off...forget about it.

'It's strange that Claudette should ring to-night, isn't it?' Sharon remarked as she leaned against the kitchen table and nonchalantly lit a cigarette.

'Is it...?' Caitlin swallowed and tried to steady her voice. 'What's strange about it? She's just a friend of Ray's.'

'A bit more than that, Caitlin—she was Ray's hostess at the last dinner party he threw for us. And they looked very much a couple.' She blew out a long curl of smoke and re-garded Caitlin through narrowed eyes. 'But then, as we all know, Ray's partners don't last very long.'

'Not until now, anyhow,' Caitlin replied coolly, infuriated by the enmity of the woman's words.

'Well, darling, only time will tell,' Sharon said, her voice almost gleeful. Then she turned and left the room.

What a bitch, Caitlin murmured to herself. But reluctantly she had to admit that, although she didn't like the woman, perhaps she had a point. Ray was a smooth operator.

She remembered her reaction to his kiss. It had been incredible. She couldn't understand why she had felt that way. Some kind of chemistry had flared between her and Ray from nowhere…and it was shocking. But what was even more shocking was the fact that no man had ever succeeded in turning her on like that before. Never had a kiss felt so explosive. The loss of control that she had experienced with Ray a few moments ago was a whole new experience and it scared her.

She took a moment to compose herself before going back through to join everyone.

Ray had just put the phone down as she stepped back into the lounge. 'Here, let me help you.' He moved to take the tray from her and as she passed it over their eyes met. Instantly flame flared inside her again. Her heart thumped unevenly against her chest, and hastily she looked away from him.

'We were just saying, Caitlin, that we would love to come and have a look at your house some time,' Roger Delaware was saying cheerfully. 'Sharon and I are going to be in the area for a couple of days, so maybe we could come and visit.'

Caitlin swallowed her dismay. 'Well, yes…but not yet. The place isn't really ready for receiving visitors and it's going to be even more of a mess tomorrow. I've got builders coming in.'

Ray watched Caitlin as she passed Roger his coffee and he tried not to think too deeply about the way she had responded to him earlier… The heat of his desire was only just starting to fade. If he dwelt on how much he wanted to take her to bed right now he was liable to throw all the guests out into the night.

He liked the way she was able to handle herself so confidently. Roger Delaware hadn't taken any offence at the subtle way she had put him off visiting her.

She laughed at something Philippe had said, her eyes sparkling with merriment for a moment as she gave a quick and funny reply.

Ray smiled. Yes, Caitlin was good to have around…a terrific hostess, very appealing to the eye…and extraordinarily sexy.

And that was when he decided that business could be put on hold until he got to know this fascinating woman much more intimately.

CHAPTER FIVE

SUN streamed in through the windows of the dining room. It was warm on Caitlin's face and for a while she lay on the sofa bed between waking and sleeping, memories from last night's dinner party drifting lazily through her mind. At the end of the evening Ray had suggested she stayed overnight rather than make the journey home. The offer had sent warning signals into orbit and she had hastily refused. After the kiss they had shared she hadn't even wanted him to drive her home, saying she would get a taxi, but he had brushed the suggestion aside and insisted on escorting her. Short of being extremely rude, she'd had to accept.

All the way back he had kept up a light conversation but she had hardly been able to concentrate on what he'd been saying. All she'd been able to think about was how she would react if he were to kiss her again. Con sequently as soon as the car had pulled up by her front door she'd jumped out and, with a cheery wave, she had rushed for the sanctuary of her house and had slammed the door tightly behind her.

Groaning at the memory, she flung back the sheets and stood up. She was annoyed with herself for allowing one kiss to spook her like that. It would have meant nothing to him at all and it should have been the same for her. So why had it kept her awake for hours last night?

The question tormented her and fiercely she tried to forget it. She didn't want to start thinking too deeply about it again today. There was too much to do. Besides, she had probably imagined the sensual intensity of the moment. Ray had just been fooling about in order to keep Sharon at a distance, and she'd had a couple of glasses of wine. The incident was best laughed off and forgotten.

She had just dressed in shorts and a T-shirt when Patrick arrived for work. Caitlin made him a cup of coffee and they chatted easily about which job to tackle first. They decided that it should be the staircase, and as Patrick unloaded his old pick-up truck and carried tools into the house to start ripping out the old set of steps Caitlin closed the doors through to the kitchen and dining room so that the dust couldn't reach her living quarters.

As work progressed in the house Caitlin went outside to try to restore some order to the overgrown garden.

The sun slowly climbed up into the azure-blue sky and by midday the heat shimmered with intense ferocity over the olive grove. Even though Caitlin was in the shade she was so hot that her throat felt raw with dryness. If the heat was like this in early spring she couldn't help but wonder what it would be like here in the summer. Hotter than Manchester, that was for sure, she thought with a grin as she took a swig of her bottled water and then climbed up a ladder that she had positioned in order to prune branches from a tree. It was hard work and she was still up the ladder an hour later with only a few branches cut when Ray arrived.

He stood at the base of the tree and admired the shapely length of her legs in the denim shorts. Her long dark hair was tied back in a pony-tail and it made her look about sixteen. For a moment he watched as she struggled on determinedly with a wayward branch that was obviously far too thick and heavy for her to cut. He noticed the small frown of concentration on her face, the way she bit her lip with pearly white teeth in vexation as the stubborn branch refused to break.

'Need any help?' he asked softly.

'Oh, hi, Ray.' She turned and looked down at him. 'I didn't expect to see you today.' She tried to make her voice light-hearted, but in truth as soon as she saw him her body seemed to tense. 'You seem to be making a habit of catching me off guard.'

'I do, don't I?' He grinned.

And suddenly she was remembering the way he had kissed her last night, the heat of his lips and the passion that had ignited so fiercely inside her.

'So, what can I do for you?' She turned her attention quickly back to her struggle with the branch, trying to saw through it with all her might.

Instead of answering her, Ray was watching what she was doing. 'You are making a mess of that,' he said.

'Am I? What am I doing wrong?'

'For a start you are using the wrong implement for the job.' He turned and searched through the old toolbox that she had found in one of the outbuildings. 'This is what you should be using.' He held up a lethal looking pair of shears.

Then to her surprise he climbed up the ladder behind her. He stood on the rung beneath her, his body pressed close behind hers. 'You see these branches here.' He leaned over her to point, his breath soft against the side of her face.

'Yes…' Desperately she tried to concentrate but his closeness was sending alarm bells ringing through her.

'They need to come out and you should always cut just about here.' He pointed to a joint in the branch, and then clipped neatly, so that the branch fell with one smooth action. In his hands the task seemed effortless. But Caitlin only vaguely registered what he was doing; all her senses were tuned in on the feeling of his body against hers, the scent of his cologne, the strength of his arms wrapped so tightly around her. The sensation was dangerously exhilarating.

'There, that should do it.' He pulled away from her and jumped down onto the ground, then held out a hand to help her down.

'Thanks.' She put her hand in his and felt as if explosive shivers raced straight from his fingers through her body.

Her feet connected with the ground but as she looked up at him she still felt as if she were falling. The world seemed to be at a crazy angle. It would be so easy to just sway closer into his arms. He was so sexy and the powerful memory of his kiss tantalised and tormented her.

Caitlin pulled away from him and mentally shook herself. She did not want to be one of Ray's conquests.

'So, what do you think of the rest of my handiwork?' she asked, looking around at the orchard and pretending to be deeply absorbed in the work she had done.

For a moment she didn't think he was going to answer her; he seemed to be studying her face very intently. 'I think…' he said carefully, slowly, 'that you have been working far too hard and should take a break and have some lunch with me.'

'I can't, Ray. I've got far too much to do.'
She moved away from him, picking up
branches to put them into a neat pile.

'Lunch doesn't take that long and you can't
work in the heat of the day.' He leaned back
against the stepladder and watched as she
moved out from beneath the tree, dusting her
hands against slender hips as she walked.

'I can.' Her hair was escaping from the con-
fines of the pony-tail and she pulled it free impatiently so that it swung down around her
shoulders.

Ray noticed that the dark chestnut colour
had gold undertones in the sunlight. For a moment he found himself wondering how it
would feel to run his hands through it as he
brought her very gently and possessively to
climax. 'You are in France now and you
should learn to do things the French way...'
he murmured distractedly.

'And what way is that?' she asked, flicking
an edgy look around at him.

'The civilised way, of course.' He smiled.

She couldn't help but smile back at him.

'Anyway, I thought you would say no to
lunch and that you'd tell me you were too
busy. So I made a contingency plan.'

'What kind of contingency plan?'

'You'll see.' Without another word he disappeared around the side of the house.

Caitlin felt a jolt of disappointment that he was leaving. Then frowned and hurriedly continued to pick up the fallen branches. She'd done the right thing passing on lunch; she needed to keep her distance from that man.

To her surprise Ray arrived back a few moments later carrying an ice box and a blanket.

'Ray, what on earth are you doing?' she asked as he spread the blanket out under the dappled shade of the olive trees.

'What do you think I'm doing?' He glanced over at her wryly. 'If you won't go to the restaurant, then I've brought the restaurant to you. The chef at Chez Louis put together an interesting menu. I hope you'll approve.'

Caitlin walked a little closer, curiosity making her lean over to look in the cooler box. She watched as he brought out an ice bucket with a bottle of white wine. 'So what else have you got in there?'

'*Salade Niçoise,* which is a speciality of the region, followed by goats' cheese and a

Mediterranean vegetable roulade, and then, to follow, a selection of fruit.'

'Sounds wonderful, but I won't be able to do any work this afternoon if I eat all that.'

Ray reached up and, catching her off balance, pulled her down onto the rug beside him. 'You know what you need, don't you?'

'No, what?' Breathlessly she watched as he poured a glass of white wine.

'You need to relax.' He pressed the glass into her hand and for a moment their eyes met across the rim.

'Well, thanks.' Quickly she looked away and held up the glass in salute. 'This is very kind of you.'

Caitlin took a sip of the wine; it had a honeyed undertone and was crisply cold. It was bliss after the busy morning in the orchard. Moving slightly so that her legs weren't touching his, she leaned back against the bark of the tree.

'Shouldn't you be working today?' she asked him.

'I always take time off for lunch.' He was unwrapping tin foil from some china plates, so she took the opportunity to study him. She noticed the muscle of his arms in the cream short-sleeved shirt, the stylish yet casual lightweight beige trousers. He looked incredibly stylish and yet there was such an air of strength about him. The pale colours he wore emphasised the dark tan of his skin and the almost blue-black hair.

He looked around, caught her watching him and smiled. 'How's the wine?'

'Delicious.'

'Try a little of this with it.' He held out a fork with some goats' cheese wrapped in crispy pastry.

After a moment's hesitation, she allowed him to feed it to her. There was something sensuous and intimate about allowing him to do that. She felt self-conscious but at the explosion of taste on her tongue she closed her eyes and gave herself up to the experience.

'What do you think?' he asked.

'Heaven…I'm sure it's the food of the gods.' She opened her eyes and smiled at him.

'Good.' He put the plates between them and some small bowls of black and green olives.

She was surprised at how hungry she was. Never had a meal tasted so amazing. Maybe it was because they were eating out of doors in the heat of the day, maybe it was the tranquil silence of the orchard, only broken by the occasional drone of a bee. Or maybe it was the company she was in. It seemed that just being around Ray sharpened all of her senses.

'The chef who put this together needs a gold medal,' she murmured as she leaned her head back against the tree and treated herself to another mouth-watering morsel. 'What did you say his name was?'

'Louis, he owns a bistro down in the village. I'll take you there for dinner one evening.'

The casual offer stirred up an anything-but-casual response inside Caitlin; she felt her stomach tighten with the kind of anticipation that had nothing to do with the thought of food.

'Well, thanks for the offer but I'm pretty busy at the moment.'

Her answer met with a moment of silence. She slanted a surreptitious glance over at him. He was lying on his side propped up on one elbow. 'You are very serious sometimes, you know,' he said lightly. 'Life is for living.'

'I know and I am living.' She grinned. 'I'm lying in my own orchard eating food prepared by a gourmet chef, a glass of wine in my hand and the heat of the sun beating down. I feel quite decadent, as a matter of fact, and more relaxed than I have in ages.'

'That's good.'

'It's just a pity I've got to get back to work.'

'Well, you are now your own boss so you could take the rest of the day off.'

'But then the garden will never get done.'

'If it makes you feel any better I have a lot of work to do this afternoon as well.'

'Do you work from home?'

He nodded. 'I have an office upstairs. I work three weeks here, one week in Paris.'

'Sounds like a good arrangement.'

'Yes, I like it.'

'I've never been to Paris.' She leaned her head back and looked up at the clear blue sky through the green tracery of branches. 'I saw the road signs for it on the drive down and was sorely tempted to make a quick detour into the centre, but I thought if I got in there I might not be able to find my way out onto the right road again.'

'You would have enjoyed the visit. It is a very beautiful city, especially at the moment with the horse-chestnut trees in bloom; the view along the Seine is magnificent.'

Caitlin took a sip of her wine. 'Well, maybe I'll go one day.'

'Come with me next week if you want. I have to go into the office most days but I'd still have time to show you the sights.'

If his invitation to dinner had caused a stir inside her, it was nothing to the reaction to this oh, so casual enticement. It caused a major landslide to her senses and the temptation to accept was powerfully strong.

When she didn't answer him immediately he shrugged. 'I suppose you are too busy working on this place.'

Something about the sardonic edge to his tone made her instantly defensive. 'Well, look at it, Ray. It needs all my attention.' She waved a hand towards the house.

'You know what they say about all work and no play?' he said lightly.

She looked away from him and swirled her wine around the glass, watching the way the sun made its contents gleam deeply gold.

'How many bedrooms has your apartment got?' She forced herself to ask the question and then glanced over at him uncertainly.

'Two. But it is not obligatory to use them both.' He watched the flush of tantalising colour over her cheekbones and smiled.

Caitlin held his gaze for a second too long and she knew without doubt that if she accepted his offer they definitely wouldn't be sleeping in separate beds and she didn't think she was ready for that. 'Yes, well, maybe I'll take you up on that some time in the future. But as I said earlier, I'm far too busy now.'

'Of course.' He smiled at her, a teasing half-smile that confused her.

'Why are you looking at me like that?'

'No reason.' He reached across and topped up her wineglass. 'I just think you are scared to relax around me. What is it, Caitlin? Are you afraid you might enjoy yourself?'

'I'm not afraid of anything.' Her heart pounded dramatically against her chest and her panic levels rose as he leaned a little closer. It made her distressingly aware that she was lying; she wasn't just scared, she was terrified. But she wasn't scared of him; she was scared of herself, of her own body's traitorous reaction to him. Because there was a wild part of her that wanted to throw caution away and say, Yes...take me out to dinner...take me to Paris...take me to bed. It was a crazy desire and the sane part of her fought it with every ounce of fortitude she could muster. Rebounding from one disastrous relationship to another was not what she needed right now.

'David and I were to be married next week.' She blurted the words out impulsively. 'And we were to honeymoon in Rome. So, you see, going to Paris with you...especially next week...just wouldn't be right.'

'Paris isn't Rome,' he said with a shrug. There was an uncomfortable silence. Then he looked at her with that penetrating gaze. 'Do you think your marriage would have worked out?'

The calm question made her frown. 'No, I don't suppose it would. But that doesn't stop the breakup hurting. We lived together for three years.'

'But he wasn't right for you, Caitlin, and when something isn't right you have to move on.' He reached out and stroked her hair back from her face so that he could see her more clearly. It was a tender gesture that brought a lump to her throat.

'How long have you been living apart?'

'Two months.' She had stormed out of the apartment on the day she had discovered the truth and had taken refuge at Heidi's house. It had been a tough few weeks, cancelling wedding arrangements, trying to untangle her finances from David's and grieving for Murdo. Caitlin took a sip of her wine and tried not think about it.

'What day should you have got married next week?' he asked casually as he started to pack away empty dishes into the basket.

'Saturday.'

'Well, if you don't want to come to Paris for the whole week, why don't you fly out towards the end of next week and join me...shall we say Friday? I'll meet you at De Gaulle airport and we can spend the weekend together, fly back together Sunday afternoon.' He turned and looked up at her. 'It will take your mind off what you would have been doing that weekend.'

It sure as hell would, she thought dazedly as she met his eyes. The thought of spending a weekend in Paris with him was like some kind of adrenalin drug that made her dizzy with confusion.

'I don't know, Ray, it's a bit soon for me to be having weekends away. But thanks for the offer.'

He grinned. 'The words "I don't know" suggest you haven't made up your mind yet. But the words "thanks for the offer" sound like a definite no. Which is it?'

'It's...' She hesitated as he moved even closer and her heart missed a beat as she noticed that his eyes were on the softness of her lips.

'So which is it?' he asked again.

'It's a definite...'

He reached over and took the glass of wine from her hands to put it down on the grass beside her and she found that she couldn't concentrate on what she was saying at all now, because he was leaning closer. 'You were saying?' He whispered the words against her ear.

'Ray, stop it...' But her tone was half-hearted and when he pulled her down to lie beside him on the rug she made barely a murmur of protest.

He smiled down at her. 'So...where were we?'

Her heart was thundering so fiercely now that she was sure he would feel it pounding against his chest as he leaned against her.

'Ray...' His lips silenced her and suddenly all coherent thought was gone. The kiss was tender and the hands that cupped her waist were gentle as he lifted her T-shirt and slid them beneath. His hands were cool against the heat of her naked skin. She could have pulled away but mortifyingly, she found she didn't have the inner strength. Instead she started to kiss him back and the sensations of wild need that raced through her body were forcefully compelling.

She longed for his hands to move higher, to touch her all over, but they remained at her waist, stroking her, tantalising her until she thought she would go out of her mind with wanting him.

His kisses were passionately sensational; it was as if he set alight some bonfire inside her that she hadn't even known existed.

He was the one to pull back and he smiled down at her lazily. 'Shall I take that as a definite yes?'

She hadn't wanted him to stop and a mixture of frustration and fury raced through her veins; frustration because she wanted to reach up and put her arms around him, tell him…no, beg him…to continue, and fury because he was so damned sure of himself.

'It was just a kiss, Ray,' she murmured gruffly. 'Don't get carried away.'

His eyes raked over her flushed countenance and the swollen softness of her lips and he grinned at that. 'I wasn't the only one who was getting carried away,' he reminded her teasingly.

She moved from him, furious with herself for responding. The guy was arrogant and overbearing and…she should have smacked him not kissed him back.

Trouble was, he was a good kisser… The shivery, delightful sensations he had stirred up inside her were still flowing around in her body now. She tried to ignore them, tried to ignore him as she stood up. But it was difficult because she was intensely aware of him.

Self-consciously, she adjusted her clothing.

'Okay, it was just a kiss…' He also got to his feet. 'But you've got to admit there is a certain chemistry between us.'

'Is there? I hadn't noticed…' Her voice trailed off huskily as he took a step closer.

'Care to put that to the test again?' He smiled as he saw the flicker of turmoil in her cat-green eyes. 'No? Well, that's a pity.'

'Stop teasing, Ray,' she muttered.

'I'm not teasing. I'm very serious. And I'm especially serious about our weekend together in Paris. In fact, to prove it to you I will offer to sleep in the spare room.' He spread his hands wide, a boyish look of contrition on his handsome features. 'Now I wouldn't do that for just anybody.'

She felt herself melt under that smile like an ice block put in the microwave.

'Yes…well, I'll think about it.' She added hastily. 'Now I'd better get inside and see how Patrick is progressing.' It was a relief to change the subject towards something mundane.

'Patrick went for lunch just as I arrived,' Ray informed her, and then added, 'He said to tell you that he would be back at four and you've got a problem with the floor.'

'What's wrong with the floor? I thought he was doing the staircase.' She shook her head.

'One problem usually begets another in these old properties, Caitlin. You'll learn that as you go along.'

'Thanks,' she grated dryly.

He grinned. 'Knowing you, you'll soon have the problem solved.' Then he glanced at his watch, picked up the picnic box and the rug. 'I've got to go. I'll speak to you later.'

'Yes…see you later.'

She watched as he disappeared around the side of the house, leaving her alone in the heat of the orchard wondering if she had just imagined the last hour.

CHAPTER SIX

'IF RAY is as attractive as you say, then I think you should go.' Heidi's voice was positive. 'What have you got to lose, Caitlin?'

Caitlin thought about the way Ray made her senses dissolve into chaos just with a smile. 'Apart from my self-control, you mean?' *And my heart,* a little voice whispered waywardly in her ear. Strenuously she ignored that. She didn't intend opening her heart again to anyone for a very long time.

'He has a weird effect on me, Heidi. I've never known anything like it. He touches me and I turn to jelly.'

'Well if some drop-dead gorgeous Frenchman wanted to whisk me off to Paris for the weekend I'd definitely go.'

'No, you wouldn't, you are happily married.'

Heidi laughed. 'Whoops, almost forgot that.'

Caitlin smiled; it was good to hear her friend's cheerful voice. She'd missed her.

'I'm just a bit wary, Heidi...'

'After what you've been through, that is understandable,' Heidi said sympathetically.

'He's not the type to want a serious relationship and that's fine... Part of me thinks it will just be a bit of fun and I should go for it. But there is another part of me that says I could get burned here. He's a smooth operator...'

'Mr Cool?' Heidi asked.

'Oh, yes, definitely Mr Cool. It's six days now since he issued the invitation and I haven't had sight or sound of him in that time. In fact I think he is in Paris now. He said he was there this week on business, so for all I know he's changed his mind about the weekend anyway.'

'Well, you've got his mobile number, haven't you? Ring him and find out.'

Caitlin frowned. She was definitely against ringing him. Why, she didn't know; maybe it was that arrogant manner of his or that laid-back confidence that said he knew he could have any woman he wanted. Well, to hell with that—she had far too much spirit to give him the satisfaction of running after him. It wasn't her style at all.

'No, I don't think that is a good idea,' she murmured. 'Anyway I'm starting to go off the idea of Paris. After all, I should have been in church this Saturday exchanging vows with David. It's too much, too soon.'

'I wasn't sure if I should tell you this or not.' Heidi hesitated. 'But Peter and I went to China Town last Saturday night for a meal, and David was in the restaurant.'

'Really?' Caitlin frowned. 'On his own?'

There was a brief pause. 'No, he was with a voluptuous blonde. And she was all over him, Caitlin, like a bad rash.'

'Oh.' A cold, raw feeling swirled inside Caitlin.

'I shouldn't have told you, should I?' Heidi said apprehensively.

'No, I'm glad you did, because stupidly I've been worried about him.'

'You are joking! Why?'

Caitlin shrugged helplessly. She couldn't explain the complex feelings she had about David. 'There was a part of me that wondered if I should have stuck around to help him. He does have a problem, Heidi—'

'You're telling me.' Heidi's voice was brusque. 'Apart from the gambling, he's a thief as well as a liar. Remind me again... How much did it cost you to extricate yourself from the mess?'

'You know very well it was a big chunk of my savings.'

'And you're worried about him?' Heidi sounded angry now. 'You are far too soft-hearted. Let me tell you, Caitlin, he didn't look one bit worried about you on Saturday night. The guy is a user.'

'Maybe you're right but...I suppose he couldn't help himself. Gambling is a bit like alcoholism, isn't it?'

'I don't know but I think you are well out of it.'

'I suppose so. I'm a disaster when it comes to picking men, aren't I?' Caitlin said wryly.

'Ray sounds all right.'

'Well, at least he's honest and up front,' Caitlin agreed. 'He's been straight about the fact he's not looking for a serious commit-ment...and he's been brutally honest about this house.' She perched herself on the window ledge, her eyes moving over the shambles that had once been the lounge. There was a hole where the staircase had been and a bigger hole where part of the floor had once been.

'Well, grab him quick and have a fab time in Paris.'

There was a sound of a car drawing up outside and Caitlin looked out of the window wondering if it was Ray. Her heart sank a little as she saw it was a van. 'I've got to go, Heidi. Someone's coming to the door. And no, it's not him.'

'Pity.' Heidi laughed. 'Don't forget to send me a postcard.'

'I might not go,' Caitlin warned as she glanced outside and noticed the logo on the van. 'Gosh, I think it might be the electricity people here to connect me. Now this is a wonderful surprise—I'd been told they could be another three weeks.'

'You see, things are looking up.' Heidi laughed. 'The future is looking bright.'

Over an hour later golden light spilled through the house and Caitlin's fridge and immersion kicked into life. She was back to civilisation. Heidi was right, she thought as she filled up the ice tray for the freezer. The future was what mattered now and she wouldn't dwell on the past. A hot bath and then an ice-cold gin and tonic beckoned.

She was just running the bath when her mobile rang again. It was an unfamiliar number not keyed into her address book, so she answered it half expecting a wrong number.

'Hello, Caitlin.'

She recognised Ray's voice immediately and she was filled with surprise and pleasure. 'Oh, hi, where did you get my number?'

'I took a note of it when I had your phone in my possession. So, how are things going with the house?' he continued swiftly.

'They are progressing well.' She closed her mind to the mess in her lounge.

'Have they reconnected your electricity yet?' he enquired.

'Well, yes, as a matter of fact they have.' She smiled. 'You must be psychic; they've just been here.'

'I'm glad things are going well for you, Caitlin.' His voice held that note of relaxed humour that made her stomach dip.

She sat down on the edge of her bath. 'So, how are things going with you? Did you get the contract with Roger Delaware all signed up?'

'Yes. He was up at the house the other day. He asked me to pass on his regards to you.'

'That was nice.' She made her voice airily light. Was he ever going to mention Paris? she wondered. And if he did, what should she say?

'I think he really wanted to call to see you.' Ray laughed. It was a warm laugh to which every sinew of her body responded positively.

'I meant to come over to see you myself, but I haven't had a minute. Work has been chaotic.'

'And I thought you French had such a relaxed attitude to work. What about those long lunches with wine?'

'They have been sadly missing. But I've been in a Paris frame of mind recently...the big city always makes me much more driven.'

'Are you there now?' she asked.

'Yes, I'm phoning from my apartment. The weather has been lovely today, a bright, cloudless blue sky...not that I've seen much of it. I've been in the office since first light.'

'That's a shame.'

'Yes, well, hopefully I'll make up for it at the weekend.'

Caitlin felt her heartbeat increase. Here it was—he was going to ask her again.

'Have you got a pen handy?'

'A pen?' She was puzzled by the request.

'Yes, I want you to take down a number.'

'I've already got your phone number.'

'Haven't used it, though, have you?' He laughed. 'No, this is a different number.'

Hastily Caitlin got up to find her bag and root through it for a pen. 'Okay fire away,' she said as she poised with her diary and pen in one hand, the phone tucked under her chin.

He reeled off a number and she wrote down. 'So what is this?' she asked as he finished.

'It's the reference number of your flight on Friday. Now, you have to be at Nice airport at five-thirty, and you collect your ticket at the Air France desk. You'll need your passport to confirm your identity.'

'You've already booked me a seat?' She didn't know whether to be cross or flattered. 'But I haven't told you if I am coming yet!'

'Well, I got impatient waiting so I booked the flight anyway. I'll pick you up at the airport. Oh, and pack a few warm clothes—although the weather is good it is a few degrees cooler than the south. I've got to go, Caitlin, I've got a call coming through on my other line.'

Caitlin opened her mouth to speak, but he had already gone. Now what should she do? she wondered restlessly. It was very presumptuous of him to just book her flight like that. By rights she should just ignore it. It would probably be the sensible thing to do.

She sighed and then looked at her reflection in the bathroom mirror. Being sensible hadn't really got her very far up to now. Maybe it was time to take a risk, live dangerously and fly to Paris. Although her heart bounced very unevenly against her chest at the thought, there was also a wave of excitement that completely engulfed her. She reached for her gin and tonic and took a deep mouthful. Roll on Friday. Whatever would be would be and she wouldn't analyse the rights and wrongs of it. She deserved a fun time anyway, after the last few weeks. Murdo would definitely approve, she thought with a grin.

The flight from Nice to Paris was short. It seemed as if the jet was no sooner up in the air than it was preparing for landing. Caitlin's stomach seemed to flip wildly as they made the steep descent into De Gaulle but she wasn't sure if it was the air pockets they hit or the fact that she was here in Paris…and a whole weekend with Ray stretched before her.

Ray spotted her immediately amidst the crowds in the arrivals hall and he smiled to himself. It had been a calculated risk just booking her ticket and he had half expected her not to turn up.

Caitlin hadn't seen him yet, but, instead of walking over to her immediately, he stopped and took the opportunity to study her as she looked around for him. The long grey skirt and matching cropped jacket she wore were teamed with black high-heel boots and a red top. They skimmed her slender body in a stylish way, making her look taller than her five-feet four. Her long dark hair was loose around her shoulders; it curled slightly at the ends and gleamed chestnut gold under the overhead lights. She looked absolutely stunning. As if sensing his gaze on her, she turned and their eyes connected across the crowded concourse. He saw the smile of relief on her face.

'I thought for a moment that I had been stood up,' she said lightly as he reached her side.

'So did I.' He grinned. 'I half expected you not to come as a punishment for my impetuosity.'

'It crossed my mind,' she admitted.

'Well, I'm glad you are here.' He smiled.

She looked up into the warmth of his eyes and she wanted to say, Me too. But the words wouldn't come out. 'Thanks for the ticket,' she said lightly instead. 'And of course I'll pay you for it—'

'Caitlin.' He cut across her firmly. 'Shut up, will you?' Then he leaned closer and suddenly she was enveloped in the warmth of his body as he kissed her lightly on each cheek. 'Welcome to Paris,' he said softly as he pulled back.

Her heart was racing so hard against her ribs that it was actually hurting her. She looked up at him wordlessly and, just as she thought he was going to pull away completely, suddenly his lips brushed against hers. It was just a light, almost teasing caress but it set clamouring fires of fierce desire instantly blazing inside her.

'So are you hungry?' he asked casually as he moved back and picked up her overnight case from beside her.

She wondered if their kisses didn't affect him as intensely as they affected her. Maybe he was used to that level of sensuality when he kissed...

Aware that he was waiting for her reply, she hastily pulled herself together. 'Eh, yes, starving, in fact,' she lied. The truth was that she was so wound up that eating was the last thing on her mind.

'Good. I know a great little bohemian restaurant on the Left Bank.'

He strode ahead of her, leaving her struggling to keep up. She noticed the way women looked at him as they wove their way through the crowds. There was open admiration in their eyes. It was no wonder they were attracted to him, she thought as he turned and waited for her by the doors. He was formidably handsome, and the dark suit he wore emphasised his stylish Parisian good looks.

They found his Mercedes in the car park and while she settled herself in the comfortable leather seats he stored her case in the trunk.

'Is it okay with you if we go directly to eat or do you want to go back to my place first?' he enquired as he slid behind the driving wheel.

'Oh, let's go and eat,' she said hastily. She wanted to put off going to his place for as long as possible; just the thought of being alone with him there made her insides tighten with a weird kind of apprehension.

They travelled in silence. Caitlin watched his hands on the wheel of the car—capable, confident hands. She tried to think of something to say, something that would take her mind off the thought of those hands travelling with equal ease and confidence over her body. But nothing came to mind.

He changed gear and the sports car roared down wide tree-lined streets. It was dark now and the cobbled streets glistened under the beam of the powerful headlights.

'You seem to know Paris pretty well,' she managed weakly at last.

'I spend a lot of time here. And I suppose you could say it is my hometown, it's the place where I was brought up. My mother was a Parisian model who worked for some of the top fashion houses. And my father was a merchant banker here.'

'Are your parents still alive?' Caitlin probed lightly.

'No, my father died when I was sixteen and my mother ten years later. She made a disastrous second marriage which ended in an acrimonious divorce. Her health was never good after that.'

'I'm sorry, Ray, that must have been awful.'

'That's life, isn't it?' He pulled the car into a vacant parking space. 'I used to blame my stepfather for making her so unhappy. But looking back I realise it wasn't entirely his fault. My mother was desperately unhappy after my father died and I suppose she was on the rebound. She was looking to recapture what she once had and that can be a dangerous route.'

She followed Ray as he stepped out onto the pavement. The night air was cool, and the pavements glistened from an earlier shower.

She wondered if that reasoning was what kept Ray a single man. Maybe he felt he'd been lucky having one good marriage and didn't want to push his luck by getting involved again. Then, realising that she was analysing him, she pushed the thought to the back of her head. Ray was single because that was the way he wanted it, she told herself sharply. And it was none of her business.

'Careful on these cobbled surfaces, they can be slippery,' Ray said as he waited for her to walk around to join him. He took hold of her hand as they waited for a space in the traffic to cross the road.

She liked the touch of his hand, cool and firm against hers.

As they rounded a corner she could see the Seine, its silky dark surface reflecting the lights of the city, its banks lit with an amber necklace of light.

'That's where we are going.' Ray let go of her hand to point down at the amber light and she realised it was a terrace overlooking the river. 'There are great views of the river from there. And the food is very good.'

'Sounds wonderful.' She smiled. 'Is this where you bring all your latest conquests?' As soon as the words left her lips she regretted them. What on earth had made her say something as crass as that?

'I wasn't aware that you were a conquest.' His eyes moved over her face thoughtfully, and then he smiled. 'Yet...'

The gentle emphasis on that last word made her blush furiously.

'Well, when I said conquest I meant the fact that I'm here in Paris with you... not...anything else.' She tried desperately to extricate herself but with each word felt she was making it worse.

He laughed and took hold of her hand again. 'Come along, Caitlin, it doesn't do to think about anything too deeply on an empty stomach. You're here and that's all that matters.'

They walked down the slip road towards the restaurant in silence. Ray opened the door for her and then stepped back to allow her to enter the building first.

It was warm inside, despite the fact that the sliding doors were open onto the terrace. Maybe the heat was generated by the amount of people, because the place was full to overflowing; people were sitting and standing at the bar area and each candlelit table seemed to be occupied. Or maybe the huge bread ovens just visible through a stone archway generated the heat. The place had a wonderful lively atmosphere, with just the right mix of sophistication and informality; the French conversations swirled around Caitlin as they made their way to the bar.

'Do you think we will get a table?' Caitlin asked. 'It's very busy.'

Before Ray could answer he was greeted by a man behind the bar who came around and embraced Ray warmly with much back-slapping approval.

For a moment they spoke in French. Caitlin was fascinated to listen to Ray speaking in his own language. If his English sounded sexy, it was nothing to the wonderful melodious tones of his native tongue.

Ray introduced her briefly to the man, who was called Henri, and he kissed her on each cheek before steering them towards the only vacant table in the place, which was strategically placed for a good view of the floodlit terrace and the river.

'You were saying?' Ray asked with a grin as the man disappeared and a waitress immediately arrived to hand them a menu.

'You've obviously got friends in high places, haven't you?' She smiled. 'Not only have you got us a table, but I think it's the best in the house.'

'Yes, well, Henri and I go back a long way. We were at school together.'

'He's the owner of this establishment, I take it?'

Ray nodded. 'He operates a system of first come, first served; you can't book a table—'

'Unless you are an old school friend,' Caitlin finished with a smile.

'Exactly.' Ray glanced down at the menu. 'So what would you like to eat?'

She looked down at the selection. It was all in French but she could make out most of it. 'What's this?' She leaned over and pointed at something she just couldn't decipher.

'Venison with sweet potatoes. Why don't you try the escargot to start with?'

'Snails?' She pulled a face and then, glancing over at him, realised that he was deliberately teasing her.

'I don't even like to look at snails in the garden, never mind eat them.'

Ray laughed. 'Then predictably I take it your choice is that most English of dishes, *Rosbif?*'

She laughed as well. 'But I'll take French mustard with it.'

'You are extraordinarily beautiful when you laugh, do you know that, Caitlin?' he said softly.

The compliment caught her off guard. There was a part of her that wanted to make a glib remark, shrug it off as nothing more than his smooth tongue. She glanced across and met his eyes; they looked dark and intensely serious and for a moment she was completely tongue-tied. It was as much as she could manage to just say the words, 'Thank you.'

He watched the flicker of uncertainty and vulnerability in her green eyes. 'David did quite a job on you, didn't he?' he remarked suddenly.

'I don't know what you mean,' she said, clearing her throat nervously.

'I mean he hurt you a great deal…took away some of that radiant confidence that sparkles naturally in your eyes and your laughter…'

She swallowed hard. 'It's been a tough few months,' she admitted lightly. 'But I'm fine now, Ray.'

He nodded. 'Well, at least being here for the weekend will take your mind off things, so we will change the subject…hmm?'

'Yes, good idea.' She smiled brightly and looked away from him pretending to study the menu in great detail. But in truth her heart was thumping erratically and it wasn't because he had mentioned David, it was the way he looked at her…the way he complimented her, the way he talked with such sincerity, as if her well-being mattered to him. It was all probably a very smooth act. But it was a wonderful one.

The waitress arrived to take their order. Self-consciously aware of Ray watching her, Caitlin ordered in French and hoped her accent sounded all right. Then Ray took over, smoothly ordering his meal and some wine.

'So how was my French pronunciation?' she asked as they were left alone again.

'You sounded fine.'

'I just wondered.' She shrugged. 'When you French speak English it sounds deliciously attractive…I wondered if the same could be said of the reverse.'

'Let me hear you again.' He rested one hand under his chin and leaned forward as if ready to catch every nuance of her tone, amusement sparkling in his eyes.

She wished now that she hadn't asked him, as with embarrassment she repeated her order.

'Hard to tell with a food order…' he murmured thoughtfully. 'Say something else.'

'What should I say?'

He grinned and pretended to think for a moment. 'You could say, Ray, I'm so pleased to be here in Paris with you… Where have you been all my life?'

'Idiot.' She grinned back at him.

'You don't care for that? Okay, let me think of something else.'

Behind them on a small stage a female gui-
tarist started to play a French love song. Its
haunting melody silenced a lot of the conversations around them, and a few people got up
to dance on the small dance floor outside on
the terrace.

'Ah, I know,' Ray said gently. 'You could
say, Please dance with me. I want to be held
close in your arms.'

She knew he was only teasing, but even so
she felt her skin heat up as he waited for her
to speak. Caitlin glanced towards the couples
on the dance floor; they weren't so much dancing as smooching and the thought of being that
close to Ray made her blood pressure increase
dramatically.

'Let me help you,' Ray murmured with a
smile, before repeating the words again in
French. Then he stood up and held out a hand.

She had no alternative but to put her hand
in his and allow him to lead the way. The floor
was packed with couples so, even if she had
wanted to, she couldn't have kept a distance
from him. Wordlessly she allowed him to pull
her close into his arms. The familiar tang of
his cologne assailed her senses. She closed her

eyes and leaned her head against his chest. The dangerous intensity of pleasure that ricocheted through her was terrifying in one way, and yet pure bliss in another.

One of his hands rested at her waist, the other on her back; she had never been more acutely aware of a man's touch before, or of the powerful body against hers. And suddenly it was as if they were alone in the room, as if time stood still. She wanted this dance to go on forever, to stay wrapped in the warm cocoon of his arms and never—ever—come back down to earth again.

As the music changed they continued to dance. Ray murmured something against her ear in French; the sound of his voice and the touch of his breath against her skin sent tingling shivers racing through her.

'I have something to tell you…my Caitlin,' he said gently in his native language.

The possessive way he used her name made her raise her head to look up at him.

He hesitated and then smiled. 'I don't know how I am going to keep my hands off you tonight,' he said slowly.

Although her French wasn't good she knew exactly what he had said. She tried to pretend she didn't, tried to just give a shrug of incomprehension. But the truth was she understood exactly what he meant…and, worse, she felt exactly the same way. She wanted him so much that it hurt inside.

'And something else,' he added in English, a warm, teasing glow in his eyes. 'You made Moules Mariniére sound like the sexiest food on the planet,' he assured her solemnly.

She laughed at that, loving him for being able to lighten the sexual intensity of the moment in such a silly, light-hearted way.

'You are crazy, you know that, don't you?' she said huskily.

'Crazy about you,' he said softly, looking deep into her eyes.

Caitlin decided to accept that remark as just light-hearted flirting, but even so it sent a tremor of delight rushing through her.

'Come on, let's go and sit down… Our food has arrived.' He pulled away from her and, keeping a light hold on her hand, led her back to the table.

As she took her seat opposite him her heart was still pounding erratically. Ray, on the other hand, seemed totally at ease. He smiled across at her and leaned over to pour her a glass of wine.

'So tell me,' he invited easily. 'How is the house *really* progressing?'

She should have been relieved that he had returned the conversation to the safety zone, but perversely her house was the last thing she wanted to talk about now. Caitlin reached for her glass and took a cooling sip of the white wine.

'The staircase is almost in.' She forced herself to concentrate. 'Patrick has been working really hard.'

'He's a decent guy.'

Caitlin nodded. 'I think he's very trustworthy. I left keys with him because he said he might come and do some work over the weekend.' She played with the food on her plate for a moment. 'There are no hard feelings, are there, Ray...about my not selling to you?'

She didn't know what made her ask that, but suddenly it seemed important.

He thought about that for a moment and wondered what Caitlin would say if he told her that her property was holding back a major development of luxury *gîtes*. And that every week that passed she was costing his company thousands of Euros. Philippe was getting very annoyed and impatient about it.

She frowned when he didn't answer her immediately and leaned forward. 'It's just that I love that house, Ray.' She spoke with passion, her eyes shining. 'It has such charm and I just know it's going to look fantastic when it's finished.'

Her infatuation with the project made him smile. 'You sound like me when I'm working on a new design,' he said. 'But if I can give you some advice, Caitlin… Never fall in love with a business project. You should be objective and unemotional at all times otherwise it could end up costing you more money than it is really worth.'

'And are you objective and unemotional at all times?' she asked meeting his eyes steadily.

'I've always tried to be in the past,' he said quietly.

Something about the serious light in his eyes, the intonation in his voice, made her wonder what was going on in his mind.

She shrugged. 'Well, I think there are more important things than money, a sense of achievement being one. And something that brings pleasure, two...' She trailed off self-consciously as she felt his eyes moving with searing intensity over her features. 'You think I'm incredibly naïve, don't you?'

He smiled at that. 'I think you are incredibly lovely,' he said easily. 'And in answer to your earlier question: no, there are no hard feelings.'

The waitress arrived to clear their table and ask if they'd like anything else.

Ray looked across at Caitlin. 'Would you like a coffee and cognac here, or shall we have them back at my place?'

The nonchalant question set Caitlin's adrenalin racing. 'Let's go back to your place,' she said softly.

CHAPTER SEVEN

IT WAS cool outside after the warmth of the bistro and Caitlin shivered slightly.

Ray put an arm around her shoulders and all of a sudden there was a different explanation for her shivers. 'Are you okay?' he asked gently.

'I'm fine.' She allowed herself to lean close to him. 'It's not really cold, is it?' she said lightly. 'It must be old age.'

'Old age?' He laughed at that. 'You are only twenty-nine.'

'What time is it?' Caitlin asked.

Ray glanced at his watch. 'Quarter past midnight.'

'Then I'm no longer twenty-nine,' she said with a sigh. 'I'm thirty. And it's damned depressing.'

'It's your birthday!' Ray stopped walking and looked down at her. 'You were going to get married on your birthday?'

She nodded. 'When I was planning it, it seemed like a mature and sensible thing to do. Thirty felt like a good age to settle down, make a commitment…'

'Not if it's to the wrong person,' Ray said gently.

'Well, with the benefit of hindsight I can see that,' she said huskily.

Ray looked down at her and wished he could see the expression on her face, but it was in shadow. He stroked a hand through her hair. 'Happy birthday, Caitlin.'

'Thank you.' She swallowed on a sudden lump in her throat. Being here with him suddenly seemed so right…as if she had come on a long and perilous journey, taken lots of wrong turnings and by sheer fluke ended up in exactly the right place. It was the strangest feeling and she couldn't really understand it. She was here for the shallowest of reasons: a bit of fun…to take her mind off things…

He reached down and then his lips met with hers and the fireworks started inside her again, and as she kissed him back all those shallow reasons for being here seemed like the thinnest tissue of lies. There was nothing superficial about her feelings for Ray. As the thoughts tried to unfold in her mind she stopped them. She wasn't going to analyse this, she told herself fiercely. This was just a light-hearted dalliance and if she tried to make it into something serious then she risked getting hurt.

It started to rain, a light, squally shower that took them both by surprise. They broke apart, laughing, and then they held hands and ran for the sanctuary of the car, but by the time they reached it the rain had passed.

Paris looked wonderful by night. They drove down wide boulevards passing floodlit fountains and impressive squares. The Arc de Triomphe looked white against the night sky, and statues of magnificent winged horses almost real as if they might fly at any moment up into the starry night. Then they were passing the Eiffel Tower, which shimmered with gold light, sending ripples of gold reflection over the Seine.

'This city is so beautiful,' Caitlin murmured.

'Yes, I think so.' Ray smiled. 'I've made a detour to get back to my place so you could see some of it. But tomorrow I'll show you around properly. And hopefully it won't rain.'

He added, softly. 'Although I can't promise anything—it is April in Paris.'

Caitlin looked across at him and smiled. 'That sounds wonderful.'

He parked the car on a quiet, leafy road. 'My apartment is just down here.' He indicated an elegant row of terrace houses. Caitlin admired their wrought-iron balconies, the intricate detail around the curve of their windows. She could just catch a glimpse of the sophisticated interiors lit by softly shaded lamps.

'Come on.' He opened the door of the car. 'Let's get inside.'

The words and the fact that she was here at his place made tension suddenly escalate inside her.

Firmly she tried to keep her mind away from the intimacy of being alone with him in his apartment. 'I half expected your city pad to be in an ultra-modern glass tower,' she said, trying to keep the conversation going in a light vein.

'I guess I'm just a traditionalist at heart.' Ray laughed. 'In fact I draw a lot of inspiration for my designs from the grandeur of bygone days. I hope you are not disappointed.'

'On the contrary, I think that's something we've got in common. I like older properties; I suppose it's one of the reasons I love Murdo's house. Restoring it almost seems like an honour.' She watched as he took her week-end case from the boot of the car. 'So you see I'm a bit of a traditionalist myself.'

The words had a hollow ring inside her. It was true; she was almost old-fashioned when it came to certain things…but she wasn't just talking about her love of period properties. For instance, she had never had a one-night stand or a casual liaison. Her relationships had all been with people she had loved…and people who she had believed loved her.

So what was she doing here? she wondered, apprehension uncoiling fully like a serpent ready to bite. Was she about to throw her rule book in the Seine and fall into bed with Ray Pascal? And if so, was she making a huge mis-take?

They walked up some steps and into a wide hallway lit by a chandelier. She watched as he collected some post from a line of five boxes in the wall. He flicked through the contents briefly, before leading the way across the white tiled floor towards the lifts. The doors were open and they stepped inside.

Ray pressed the button for the top floor. The overhead lights were bright and she noticed the way rain still sparkled in the darkness of his hair, and suddenly she was filled with the urge to reach out and brush her hand lightly over the dampness, smooth it away. The temptation startled her almost as much as the sudden rain shower had done a little while ago. It sent vibrant heat flooding through her.

He glanced over and met her eyes. Their dark, sensual power made the heat increase even more, and that made her even more nervous.

She cleared her throat. 'I take it you haven't been home today?' she asked, indicating the mail in his hand.

'No, I headed straight from the office to pick you up at the airport.'

'You must be tired.' It was just something to say, but as soon as the words left her lips she regretted them, especially as she saw the gleam of amusement in his dark eyes.

'Not really,' he assured her wryly.

'Well, it's been a long day for both of us.' She brushed at an imaginary crease in her grey skirt and studied the black leather of her boots as the lift slid smoothly to a halt.

She felt like a gauche teenager on a first date... This was ridiculous, she told herself crossly.

The doors opened and she followed him out of the close, confined space with a degree of relief. At least the lighting along the hallway was more subdued. He unlocked a door and led the way inside.

The apartment was elegant and spacious. The floors a highly polished maple and the leather sofas a squashy vanilla cream; in fact everything about his home spoke of style, sophistication and money.

'It's a beautiful apartment.' She crossed to the French windows to look out. There was a small roof-top garden outside. Ray flicked a switch and the space was lit with the twinkle of subdued lighting, illuminating the flower pots and the wrought-iron table and chairs. In the background the city of Paris glittered like a million priceless diamonds. 'You have a wonderful view as well.'

'Yes, I just don't get much time to admire it.' Ray tossed his post down onto an antique sideboard as he crossed to switch on a few more lamps around the sides of the room. 'Would you like to freshen up while I get us a drink?' he asked.

'Yes, okay.'

'I've put you in my room. I thought you would be more comfortable in there.'

Caitlin turned from the window and their eyes met. She wondered what it would be like to share that room with him...to lie in his arms, drown in his kisses. Urgently she tried to ignore the electric feeling of desire that sizzled inside her. She shouldn't have come here an insistent voice warned her. Maybe she should leave while she still had some semblance of sanity. 'I feel very guilty turning you out of your bedroom, Ray, especially as you've had such a busy day.' Her words came out in a rush. 'You know, I can still go to a hotel... There must be hundreds around here.'

'Hundreds.' He agreed. He leaned back against the sideboard and regarded her with a lazily amused grin. 'But the agreement was that you stayed here and, as I am a man of my word, I wouldn't hear of you disappearing off to a hotel.'

'Thank you.' There was little else she could say, but deep down she wondered if she should still have insisted on going to a hotel anyway. Ray probably was a man of his word, but it was her own strength of spirit that worried her. One look from him and she felt her self-control melting...one kiss and her mind started to wander.

'The bedroom is this way.' Ray turned and led her down a small corridor and up some steps. The room he showed her into was very luxurious; a massive bed dominated the centre. It was probably the biggest bed Caitlin had ever seen and it was covered in plain cream linen that echoed the colour of the curtains and the carpet.

'Bathroom is through there.' Ray put her bag down and indicated a door at the far end of the room. 'We'll have a coffee and cognac out on the terrace if it's still dry.'

'Thanks.' As soon as the door closed behind him she sank down onto the bed. She should have told him she didn't want a drink... In fact the safest thing would be to hide in here and not come out until it was time for her flight on Sunday.

She smiled to herself. 'Coward,' she mocked herself silently. And then, annoyed with herself, she got up from the bed and took her cosmetic bag into the bathroom.

Her reflection stared back at her from several mirrors over the basin and the bath. She looked a little pale and her green eyes seemed to swamp her small face. 'Just have a drink with him and then retire for the night,' she told herself sensibly. 'You've never had any difficulty saying no to a man before, why should Ray be any different?' But deep down she knew that, whatever the reason, Ray was different and she didn't want to say no. Certainly David had never swept her senses into such tumultuous turmoil.

She wondered what David would be doing today… Would he think about the fact that this should have been their wedding day? Maybe not, maybe he would be too busy enjoying himself with the mysterious blonde Heidi had seen him with. She hoped sincerely that, whoever he was with, and whatever he was doing, he had taken her advice and sought counselling for his addiction.

Hastily she refreshed her make-up, brightened her lipstick and ran a comb through her hair. After the rain it was curling more and she gently teased the ends so that they were soft and loose around her face.

There, that was better. She stepped back and looked at herself, then smiled. She was going to just relax and enjoy herself and not think too deeply about anything.

There was music playing in the lounge when she went back through. But Ray wasn't in the room. She glanced out onto the terrace. It was raining again, fat drops of water were bouncing on the table.

'I'm in here,' Ray's voice called her from a room off the lounge. She followed the sound and found him in his office, sitting on the edge of a writing bureau, reading through some of his mail. There were two glasses of brandy sitting next to him. 'Sorry.' He picked a glass up and held it out to her as she came in. 'I got sidetracked. I'll make coffee now.'

'No, that's okay.' She came closer and took the drink. 'I'm happy with just the brandy.'

She glanced at the in-tray next to him, which was full to the brim. 'You look like you've got a lot of correspondence to get through.'

'A week's worth of faxes. It's always the same when I'm back here—I spend all my time catching up on the correspondence I've missed. A lot of it is junk, of course, but I have to wade through it just in case.'

'You could do with a secretary.' Caitlin perched next to him on the desk and sipped her drink.

Ray was still perusing the letter in his hand. 'Yes...I have one at the office, of course.' Despite the fact that he answered her, she knew he was only half listening.

Caitlin glanced around the room. Although this was a place of work, it had a cosy feel to it with its book-lined walls at one side and subdued soft lighting. There was a daybed in one corner and above it some beautiful paintings of Paris.

She wandered over to have a look at them. 'These are impressive.' She glanced over at him but he barely looked up.

'And it's a lovely office,' she commented, sitting down on the daybed. 'You could use it as a spare bedroom.'

She had his attention now. He put the letter down and looked over at her with a grin. 'I'm going to tonight. That's unless I get a better offer, of course,' he added roguishly.

'Oh...I see!'

Ray watched as her skin coloured slightly and he smiled.

'It's quite a comfortable bed,' Caitlin continued hastily, trying to cover her embarrassment.

'You think so?' he asked, one dark eyebrow raised wryly.

'Definitely.' She bounced slightly as she tested the mattress. 'I'll trade with you if you want and you can have your own bedroom back.'

He shook his head. 'That wasn't the kind of offer I had in mind,' he said softly.

The words sent a tremor of awareness shooting through her. She glanced over at him and met the teasing gleam of his eye. 'You are one smooth operator, Ray Pascal,' she said lightly.

'Now what makes you say that?' He laughed.

'Because you just are.' She stood up from the bed and walked back towards the desk. 'And I've been warned about you.'

'Who by?' he asked with amusement.

'Sharon, for one.' She stopped a few feet away from him.

'Now what would Sharon know about anything?' Ray reached and took hold of her arm and pulled her closer, then he took her glass and put it down beside his on the desk.

'Well, she was able to tell me all about the rapid turnover of women in your life and she knew who Claudette was.'

'All Sharon knows is that I've never taken her to bed—nor would I ever want to.'

Caitlin grinned. 'She would be devastated if she heard you—'

'Well, I'm not going to lose any sleep over that,' he said gently. 'This is how it is,' he said solemnly, looking into her eyes. 'Claudette is in the past, David is in the past and at the present it's just you and me and one very uncomfortable daybed.'

She smiled tremulously, her heart starting to race as he pulled her even closer.

'That's all right, then,' she whispered huskily. 'Because the present is all I'm interested in right now.' Then she leaned forward and to her surprise she found herself making the first move, touching her lips against his in a tentatively gentle caress. He didn't respond immediately and she moved closer, her hands resting on his shoulders as she deepened the kiss provocatively.

For a little while Ray allowed Caitlin to dictate the pace; he returned her kisses with restraint, reining himself back with supreme control.

Caitlin's lips became more and more persuasive, her hands moving to thread their way through the darkness of his hair. She wanted him so much, longed for his kisses to deepen the way they had before.

Then suddenly he started to return her kisses more forcefully, his lips demanding and hungry against hers. She revelled in the feeling, her whole body tingling with need. But as she slipped further and further into the whirlpool of pleasure he suddenly pulled back from her. 'Are you sure about this?' he asked huskily. 'It's just if we carry on like this I'm not going to be able to pull back. I've only got so much self-control, Caitlin.'

Her heart quivered unsteadily. From the moment she had leaned over and kissed him the fires had started inside her and they refused to be dampened now. 'So have I,' she admitted softly. 'Make love to me, Ray.'

He smiled and she saw the sudden flare of triumph in his dark eyes. Then he reached and started to unbutton her red top, his fingers brushing lightly against her skin making her tremble inside with chaotic need.

'What about all those strong words,' he murmured playfully as he looked into her eyes, 'about sleeping in separate beds...hmm?' As he spoke the red top was pulled off.

'They were strong words...weren't they?' Caitlin murmured, her eyes closing on a wave of ecstasy as his hands moved over the lace of her bra, his fingers touching lightly against the hardened peaks of her breasts. 'And they got me here, didn't they?'

He found the fastener at the front of the black bra and toyed with it provocatively. 'So no more talk of separate beds, then?'

'Not for now...' She was desperately anxious for him to just carry on caressing her. She didn't want to talk. He was sitting on the desk and she was held between his knees; they tightened against her thighs.

'That's not a good answer,' he drawled teasingly. 'You should have said, No more talk of separate beds, I promise, Ray.'

'You are just a tease, Monsieur Pascal,' she murmured, half annoyed, half amused by his demands.

'It takes one to know one,' he said with a smile, his fingers moving to the zip at the back of her skirt. He unfastened it and pulled the skirt down, letting it fall to the floor, so that now she stood before him in only her underwear, black boots and lace top stockings.

'Nice outfit,' he murmured, his eyes moving boldly over her.

The possessive way he looked at her made her senses race; it was almost as if she could feel his eyes touching her. 'So am I the only one getting undressed here?' she murmured huskily and reached to start unbuttoning his shirt. As it opened she slid her hands beneath the material, stroking over the powerful contours of his chest.

He leaned forward and kissed her; it was a kiss that was so passionate it made her body dissolve with need. She wound her arms tightly around his shoulders and kissed him back wildly. The next moment he was lifting her up and turning her so that she was the one sitting on the desk. He swept the papers and the glasses roughly to one side and some of the paperwork tumbled to the floor but neither of them even noticed the chaos around them, they were entangled in an embrace that shut everything else out.

Caitlin was only vaguely aware of the cool surface of the desk against her back as she lay against it. All she could think about was the bliss of his hands against her skin, the heat of his lips as he kissed the sensitive areas of her neck and then her shoulders.

He unfastened her bra and then his lips moved downwards to tease the rosy hard peaks of her breasts. She gasped with pleasure as she felt his hand moving the delicate lace of her panties so that he could explore her more thoroughly.

'Ray, I want you so much.' She murmured the words almost incoherently, desperate now with a longing that was tearing into her with searing intensity.

He lifted her up from the desk as if she were a mere doll and she wrapped her legs around his waist as he carried her over to the bed in the corner.

'We may as well make ourselves a little more comfortable,' he said as he placed her down gently against the satin cushions.

She watched as he took his shirt off and then hastily she unzipped her boots and rolled down her stockings. When she looked up she found he was watching her, a gleam of naked desire in his dark eyes.

'God, you are so gorgeous, Caitlin.'

He stroked his hands along the shapely length of her legs as she leaned back against the cushions. He was gorgeous too, she thought hazily. He had an incredibly beautiful body, wide shoulders, lithe hips, a flat stomach and an arousal that made her heart start hammering with even more force.

The only item of clothing she wore now was her lacy black panties and he played with the delicate string of material for a moment before pulling them firmly down, then he moved to kneel over her. His eyes raked over her, taking in the way her hair spilled over the gold cushions behind her head, the flush of heat on her skin, the soft pout of her lips, then moved lower, examining her curves as if committing them to memory.

He touched her breasts softly, exploring the full roundness, his thumb rasping slightly against the sensitive hardness of her nipples. She shivered and closed her eyes on a wave of ecstasy. Waiting for him was like a pleasurable kind of torture; every nerve, every inch of her skin was aching. She reached up and put her hands on his shoulders, urging him silently to come closer.

And then she felt the full force of his arousal pressing against her and suddenly he was inside her. The feelings of pleasure were so vehemently intense that she gasped.

'Are you okay?' he murmured, stroking her hair tenderly back from her face, his movements gentle.

'I'm more than okay.' She smiled up at him, loving his tenderness. Then she moved her hips provocatively and drew him closer. She felt greedy with need; it was eating her alive. She wanted him with an impatience she had never known before. Ray grinned and bent down to nuzzle his lips in against her neck and her ear.

'Patience, my sweet...' he whispered softly and then spoke in French. His words were teasingly provocative as he skilfully brought her again and again to the brink of climax. She clung to him, pressing her lips against the warmth of his skin, moaning with pleasure, wanting the joy to go on and on forever and yet at the same time desperate for the ultimate sensation of release.

Ray was a skilful lover. He knew exactly how to please a woman. He teased and tormented her, showing her the dizzying heights of passion, his lips ravishing her body, his hands caressing her with the smooth ability of experience. Then just when she thought she could stand it no longer he took full possession again and brought her to the wild heights of a bliss that splintered inside her in wave after wonderful wave of fulfilment.

She clung to him afterwards, wrapped in the warmth of his arms, so exhausted she couldn't even think coherently, never mind talk. He soothed her tenderly as if she were a babe in his arms and whispered sweet nothings against her ear.

Caitlin cuddled closer. She felt as if she could never get close enough to him, as if she wanted to melt into his very skin. She had never known the ache of such a longing…or the wonder of such sweet content.

Then his lips found hers and he kissed her again, this time without the fierceness of hunger and with all the tenderness of a sated lover…

Caitlin groaned and wound her arms around his shoulders. She wanted to tell him how much she loved him…how desperately she wanted him…that she would do anything for him. The thoughts tumbled through her mind in wild confusion before exhaustion took her over and she fell into the peaceful oblivion of a deep sleep.

CHAPTER EIGHT

WHEN Caitlin woke she was disorientated. She was wrapped in a tangle of white sheets. Across from her on the opposite wall she could see bookshelves; everything was unfamiliar to her sleep-blurred eyes. She stretched and every part of her body felt stiff. Then suddenly the memories from last night unfurled in her mind in a red-hot reel of Technicolor. The way she had almost pleaded with Ray to make love to her, the way he had undressed her at his desk...the way he had lazily and skilfully brought her to climax amidst the cushions of this bed.

Then she remembered the way he had woken her in the night to take her again, and the way she had met his demands with fiery acquiescence, loving the hotly possessive touch of his lips and hands against her body. Her stomach muscles tightened as a wave of renewed hunger hit her.

But the memory that disturbed her most was of the feelings that had accompanied the wild, reckless lovemaking...the emotions that had driven her, the words that she hadn't dared speak... She frowned and pushed a trembling hand through her hair... At least she hoped she hadn't spoken them. It was disturbing enough that all her inhibitions had been totally stripped—and that Ray knew her body was completely his for the taking—without letting him know that her heart had also somehow been thrown in with the package.

She stared up at the ceiling and told herself in very angry terms that her feelings of love had been a mistake...an illusion. Last night was about having fun—two consensual adults letting their hair down. If Ray thought for one moment that she was attaching more importance than that to it, he'd be horrified. And she wasn't, she told herself fiercely. She didn't know where those mad thoughts had come from. Maybe it was because no man had ever made her feel so wonderful...so wanton, so pleasured...and she was confusing mind-blowing sex with love... That could explain it, she told herself with conviction.

The sound of a drawer closing made Caitlin aware suddenly that she wasn't alone in the room. She sat up slightly and looked down towards Ray's desk.

Early morning sun slanted through the slatted blinds. It fell over the discarded clothes on the floor. Her skirt was in a heap at the foot of his desk, her bra was sitting in the in-tray…her lacy pants were in the middle of the floor. Embarrassment ate through her.

Then the chair behind the desk swivelled around as Ray turned from the filing cabinets. He was wearing a thick white towelling robe, his dark hair was tousled and there was the beginning of dark designer stubble on his square jaw.

Their eyes met and he smiled. 'Good morning, sleepyhead,' he said tenderly and at the sound of his voice and the sexy glint in his dark eyes she felt all her strong words melt into confusion… She couldn't ever remember feeling so overwhelmed by a man before; he was just sensational.

'Morning.' She smiled back at him. 'What time is it?'

'Seven forty-five.'

'Gosh, so early!' She stretched again and sat up further, taking care to keep the sheets firmly in place so that her nakedness was covered. 'What are you doing?' she asked.

'We made a bit of a mess of my paperwork last night.' He glanced across at her again and grinned as he noticed the blaze of heat on her cheekbones. 'So I thought I'd sort it out and do a bit of work while I'm at it. Then we can go out and enjoy the day.'

'Sounds like a good plan.'

She wanted to get out of bed but she was embarrassed by her nakedness… Absurd, considering the fact that he had seen and sampled every naked inch of her body last night, but she couldn't help it—in the cool light of day she was suddenly shy again.

'I think I might go and have a shower,' she said hesitantly.

'Mmm, good idea. I'll follow you once I've finished here.'

Did he mean he intended to follow her into the shower itself? she wondered heatedly. Or did he just mean that he was allowing her to use the bathroom first?

Caitlin wasn't used to being in such close quarters with a man she knew so little about. All right, she knew his body very well now…and she had been as intimate with him last night as it was possible to get. But apart from the fact that she knew he found her attractive and that they were sexually compatible, she didn't know what else was going on in his mind. It made her feel awkwardly inept as to how to handle this situation. It made her almost wish that she had more experience in casual affairs.

Gathering her courage, she wrapped the sheet around her toga-style and stepped out of the bed. She could hardly dash from the room while all her clothes were scattered about the place in wild abandonment, so she stooped to pick up a few things. Her panties and stockings from the floor were first to be snatched up. Then she approached his desk and picked up her skirt and the bra from his in-tray.

She didn't dare look at him as she did this, but she was aware of him watching her. Then as she made to turn away from the desk he reached out and caught hold of her arm.

'Don't I get a good morning kiss?' he asked gruffly.

Her stomach turned over as she met his eyes, and she allowed him to steer her around the side of his desk where he pulled her down onto his lap.

'There, that's better.' He smiled, his eyes on her lips. 'Last night was very enjoyable.'

'Yes...' She felt breathlessly helpless. All she wanted was for him to fold her into his arms again and do exactly what he had done to her last night. The lack of all control scared her. She needed to be careful around him; her emotions were all over the place. The wild feelings of love last night worried her especially. She was still raw from her breakup with David and she couldn't trust her feelings.

He noticed the flicker of uncertainty and vulnerability in her green eyes and then as she tried to avert her gaze his finger firmly lifted her chin so that she was forced to look at him.

'You are an incredibly sexy woman,' he murmured. Then his lips met with hers in a warmly seductive kiss and the fire ignited inside her with such ferocity that it swept her mind away all over again. He laced his hands through her hair, holding her still while his mouth explored hers with compelling sensuality, then his hands moved to the sheet that covered her, pulling it away so that his hands were free to move over the smooth velvet nakedness that lay beneath. His fingers found her breasts, caressing and toying with her as his lips trailed a heated path down her neck and lower. The slight rasp of his skin against the softness of hers was somehow incredibly sexy, adding to the intense desire welling up inside her.

As his lips found the sensitized warmth of her breast she gasped and closed her eyes, the clothes that she had gathered from the floor slipping from her fingers as her hands moved to rake through the darkness of his hair. She buried her face into its softness, breathing in the scent of him, the tang of cologne and soap.

The sudden shrill ring of the phone behind them made him stop abruptly. Her heart was thundering against her chest; she wanted to tell him not to answer it, but to carry on. Her eyes met with his, wide and silently pleading for more of his kisses...much more of his caresses.

And for a moment she thought he was going to oblige and that he was as impatient to continue as she was. Then the answer machine came on. 'Hi, Ray, it's Sadie…I need to speak to you.' She spoke in French, her voice huskily attractive. 'Can I see you today or is that not convenient? It's just…' Anything else she was saying was cut off abruptly as Ray swung the chair around and picked up the receiver.

'Hello, Sadie.' As he spoke he watched Caitlin gather the sheet around her body. 'No, today isn't suitable… Yes, that's why I left the office early yesterday.'

Caitlin slipped from his knee and bent to pick her clothes up again. Their eyes met as she stood up. 'I'm going to go have that shower,' she mouthed.

He nodded.

As Caitlin left the room his conversation continued. She closed the door behind her and told herself that it was just as well they had been interrupted; it gave her time to gather her senses. The words fought valiantly with the red-hot need that still swirled inside her, refusing to be extinguished.

She made her way back to her bedroom and threw her clothes down on a chair. The massive bed, still pristinely untouched, seemed to mock her. So much for hiding in here all night, she thought wryly, so much for being in control of the situation.

Leaving the sheet on the floor, she went through to the bathroom and turned the shower on full. Standing under the razor-sharp jets of hot water, she washed her hair and soaped her body with hard, vigorous strokes in the vain attempt to rid herself of the need that was still rampaging through her.

Caitlin didn't like the feeling of being out of control. It was important that she took stock of things now; emotionally distanced herself from the heat Ray stirred up inside her.

Then the shower door opened and Ray stepped in beside her and suddenly the thought of distancing herself was the furthest thing on her mind.

'Now where were we?' he murmured with a grin as he took her firmly into his arms.

Hours later as they wandered along the Champs-Elysées, gazing into designer boutiques, Caitlin was still trying to close her mind on the steamy hot passion they had shared to-gether earlier. But it seemed to colour the whole day. It was there in the heat of the sun that shone down on them, it was there in the white intensity of the blossom on the trees, in the swirling silky darkness of the Seine. And it was fiercely present every time Ray looked at her or smiled, or touched her. The emotions she so wanted to suppress were out of control, and as much as she tried, she couldn't seem to get them back into the neat little compartment where she could shut the lid on them.

Was she on the rebound? she wondered as Ray insisted on dragging her into a jewellery shop to look at a necklace she had admired in the window.

Maybe…she was…

'You must try it on.' Ray cut through her thoughts as he lifted the amber necklace from its velvet case.

'No, really, Ray. I think it's very pretty but—'

'Lift your hair up,' he cut across her with a smile. 'And I'll fasten it for you.'

She found herself doing as he asked. Even the touch of his fingers against her skin as he fastened the gold chain made her senses swim.

'So what do you think?' he asked as the assistant brought a mirror so Caitlin could see herself.

She released her hair and glanced at herself. The necklace looked fantastic against her skin, its amber colour reflecting the amber lights in her hair and bringing out the green-gold of her eyes.

'It's looks wonderful, doesn't it?' Ray said softly. He leaned forward and kissed her cheek and for a moment they were both reflected in the oval mirror. Caitlin couldn't help thinking that they looked right together somehow. The thought was crazy and she moved away from him slightly and reached to unfasten the necklace.

'You should keep it on.' He caught hold of her hand before she could find the catch. 'It complements the black trouser suit you are wearing perfectly.' He nodded at the assistant who took the mirror away. And then the next moment Ray was passing a credit card across the counter.

'No, Ray, I can't let you buy it!' Caitlin was horrified. She had been so busy daydreaming earlier that she hadn't been fully aware of the price of the piece. 'It's far too expensive.'

'You like it. Don't you?' he asked nonchalantly.

'Well, I love it, but—'

Ray was already signing on the dotted line. 'It's a birthday present,' he said. 'And I want you to have it.'

The sales assistant gave him his receipt and smiled at them both. Caitlin noticed how she particularly smiled at Ray…but then it was the same everywhere they went—women just seemed to fall over themselves for him.

'Thank you, Ray, but you shouldn't have done that,' she told him as they made their way back outside. 'It's far too generous a gift.'

'No, it's not.' He caught hold of her hand and smiled at her. 'Besides, I have an ulterior motive.'

'You have?' She looked over at him uncertainly.

'Yes.' He leaned closer and kissed her softly on the lips. 'I want you to undress for me later and wear it as I make mad, passionate love to you.'

The wild rush of adrenalin inside her seemed to scorch through her skin. 'I think that could be arranged,' she said huskily, and there was part of her that wanted to ask if they could go back to his apartment right now.

'Good.' He pulled a strand of her hair playfully. 'But now I think we should go and have something to eat.' He raised a hand to flag down a taxi.

Ray took her to a small restaurant in a lovely old square and they sat at a table outside and sipped some wine as they perused the menu.

He glanced across at her and smiled and her heart seemed to do an alarming somersault. If she was on the rebound, then how come these emotions were so much more intense than they had been with David the first time around? The question snaked its way into her thoughts. No one had ever made her feel like this before.

'So have you decided?' he asked as a waitress came out to take their order.

She glanced quickly back down at the menu. She had decided, she reminded herself firmly, not to think about anything too deeply any more.

After the waitress took their order they sat in companionable silence. It was interesting watching the people walking across the square; some were obviously tourists because they posed for photographs outside the small chapel opposite. Some were Parisians, smartly dressed going about their daily business, and others were lovers strolling hand in hand in the sunshine.

For a moment Caitlin found herself thinking about her wedding and she glanced at her watch. It was almost three. She would have been arriving at the church now.

And it probably would have been the worst mistake of your life, a little voice reminded her sharply.

Watching her, Ray noticed how she looked at her watch and how her skin suddenly blanched. Was she thinking about the wedding and David? he wondered.

'Are you okay?' he asked softly.

She glanced across at him and smiled, and suddenly the pain inside her started to subside.

'I'm absolutely fine,' she told him sincerely.

It was late by the time they got back to his apartment.

They had sailed down the Seine on the Bateaux Mouches, admiring the fine architecture of the city. They had taken the lift to the top of the Eiffel Tower and they had sat at a pavement café at Montmartre as darkness had stolen over the city.

The plan had been to shower and change and go out for dinner. But once in the privacy of the apartment the plans were somehow forgotten as they ended up tumbling into bed, to make wild, passionate love.

At ten-thirty they awoke in the darkened apartment and both were ravenously hungry. So Ray phoned for a take-away and opened a bottle of champagne. They picnicked on the roof terrace, admiring the twinkle of the Parisian lights.

'Life is strange, isn't it?' Caitlin reflected as she sipped the champagne. 'If someone had told me a few months ago that I would be spending my birthday in Paris with you, I wouldn't have believed them.'

Ray grinned. 'What is it they say…? Life is what happens when you are busy making other plans.'

'That's very true.' Caitlin sipped her champagne and the bubbles went up her nose.

'What happened between you and David?'

The quietly voiced question took her by surprise.

Ray watched her silently for a moment and noticed the flicker of vulnerability in her wide green eyes. Then she looked away from him.

When they had got out of bed she had thrown on a white silk blouse and a pair of jeans. Her hair was tousled around her face and very sexy; her skin still had a glow across her cheekbones that a moment ago had been due to the wild heat of their lovemaking... And now probably was down to the fact that she was uncomfortable with his questions.

'It just didn't work out, Ray,' she said lightly.

'Was there another woman?'

'No!' Her skin held even more heat now. 'I think maybe I could have coped with that better,' she added impulsively. 'At least I could have hated him for that...' She shrugged and then added huskily, 'Instead there is this horrible feeling that I failed him...because I wasn't able to help him.' She looked over at

Ray and her eyes shimmered with a different raw emotion for a moment. 'But how can you help someone when they won't admit they have a problem, when they refuse to even talk about it in terms of a problem? He had a serious gambling addiction, but he refused to see it that way.'

'I see,' Ray said quietly. 'A lot of addicts are like that and if they are not ready to accept help there is very little you can do.'

Caitlin shook her head. 'I probably didn't handle it very well. When I found out I was shocked and angry and I moved out. But afterwards when I'd calmed down I tried to talk to him. I got all the leaflets, you know, about places to call and counselling services, but he was furious with me for even suggesting it. He thought we should just go on as if it didn't matter—it was just a hobby, he said.' Caitlin toyed with her glass. 'Taking my engagement ring off was a last resort…but even then he thought I was the one in the wrong.'

'You still care about him a lot, don't you?' Ray said softly.

'Of course I care about him, and I'm worried about him. We were together for three

years, and it's hard to switch off from that...'
She trailed off huskily. Then she glanced over
at him and their eyes met and a red-hot wash
of emotion swept through her. Although it was
true, she did care about David, it was nothing
to the explosive feelings that Ray could stir up
inside her.

The acknowledgement sent shock waves
through her and hastily she took another sip of
her drink. She wasn't thinking straight, she
told herself fiercely.

'So, anyway, that's the sorry state of my ro-
mantic entanglements.' She forced a light note
to her voice and gave him a half-smile. 'What
about you?'

He shrugged. 'Since Hélène died I have
found it easier to avoid entanglements. I've
kept my relationships light and my workload
heavy.'

'And that's what you recommend for a broken heart, is it?' It was difficult to sound de-
tached. She knew that her time here with him
was just a casual fling, but she didn't like it
pointed out in such cool terms.

'No, I wouldn't recommend that...' For a
moment he was silent. She glanced over at him

and noticed how his eyes seemed shadowed with sadness. 'I can't say that it has helped heal the pain of losing her.'

She swallowed hard, suddenly ashamed that she had made such a flippant remark. 'I'm sorry, Ray.'

He shook his head. 'I've come to terms with Hélène's death...I've had to. But I still miss her.'

Caitlin drew her legs up onto the chair and hugged her knees close in against her chest. 'Tell me about her,' she invited softly.

'What do you want to know?' He looked amused for a moment.

Caitlin shrugged. 'Where did you meet? What was she like?'

She rested her chin on her knees and watched him as he spoke.

'We met in Provence at the château. My mother had relocated down there after my father died and she was having the place redecorated. I had just graduated from university and was only there for a short visit before starting a new job in Paris. Then Hélène walked in with her team of decorators in tow. She looked incredible with her dark hair billowing around her face, like something from a pre-Raphaelite painting. Dark eyes, pouting soft lips that were quick to smile, she oozed life and vitality. My four-day break stretched into a two-week stay. I only just made it back in time to start my job. Then two weeks later I had persuaded her to give up her interior design job and move up to Paris to live with me.'

'Wow,' Caitlin said softly. 'It must have been love at first sight.'

Ray nodded. 'I had never been a great believer in that before. But yes it was like a bolt of lightning...*coup de foudre*...I can still see her very clearly in my mind just as she was that day when she walked into the château, still remember the feelings she stirred up inside me. We were married two months later. There were a few raised eyebrows that everything was happening so quickly.' He shrugged. 'But we just knew it was right, and I'm glad now that we didn't waste time...'

'How long were you together?' Caitlin asked softly.

'Seven years, and they were good years.' He shrugged. 'So that is something to be happy about. I went into partnership with Philippe and as the business took off we were able to spend more and more time down in Provence. Hélène always loved it down there, it was home for her. At first we were just there for the month of August when everything shut down in Paris. But then later, after my mother died and I inherited the château we would spend longer there.'

He fell silent for a long moment. 'And that was where she died, down in Provence where it all started... She lost control of her car on one of the hairpin bends going down to the village.'

'I'm sorry, Ray...'

For a moment he looked as if he hadn't heard her, then he glanced over at her and shrugged. 'Life goes on, doesn't it Caitlin? And you learn to just get on with things.' His voice seemed hard suddenly.

Caitlin reached across and covered his hand with hers. She didn't know what to say to him; words somehow seemed so inadequate.

He smiled at her. 'Anyway, enough of this maudlin talk,' he said, his mood lightening in an instant as he pulled away from her touch and refilled her champagne glass.

'Let's drink to the future, shall we?' He raised his glass.

She had just taken a sip of the sparkling wine when the sound of the phone ringing in the apartment disturbed them.

'I won't be a moment.' Ray lifted his glass and brought it inside with him, leaving Caitlin to gaze out over the city and reflect on his words.

Her breakup with David had been raw and difficult but next to Ray's loss it seemed to pale into insignificance.

It was obvious that Ray was still deeply in love with his late wife; it was there in his voice, in his eyes.

A cool breeze whispered over the terrace, sending the wind chimes ringing. Caitlin shivered a little and then decided to clear the table.

As she came back out of the kitchen she could hear the deep, melodious tone of Ray's voice as he spoke in French. On impulse she went and stood by the office door to look in at him.

He was sitting in his chair behind the desk, but he didn't see her because it was swivelled sideways as he riffled through some papers he was taking from a filing cabinet. The phone was balanced between his ear and shoulder as he spoke. It was clearly a business call.

I've kept my relationships light and my workload heavy. Ray's words echoed inside her mind and she felt a tinge of pain as she thought of them. Then hastily she turned away from the door. She needed to do the same thing, she told herself sternly.

Out of the corner of his eye Ray glimpsed Caitlin as she moved away from the door. He raked a hand through his hair impatiently. 'Look, Philippe, it is nearly midnight and I don't want to talk about this now. For one thing I have Caitlin here with me. Let's leave it at least until Monday.'

'Time is money, Ray. We need to sort this out as soon as possible.' His business partner's voice was insistent. 'The solicitor faxed me a copy of Murdo's will this morning. It makes interesting reading.'

'Yes, Sadie rang to tell me all that this morning—'

'But I've had my solicitor look through it since then,' Philippe cut across him swiftly. 'And there is a way around the problem of

Caitlin not being allowed to sell the place for six months.'

'Go on.' Ray leaned his head back against his chair resignedly.

'You could marry her.'

The softly spoken words made Ray sit up as if he had been shot. 'You are joking, Philippe!'

'No, I'm deadly serious. Murdo has made special provisions for it, even named you in the will. If you marry Caitlin the property will be yours straight away, lock, stock and barrel, as they say, and he has even placed some money in trust as a wedding present for you both. I'm telling you, Ray, if you marry Caitlin there would be nothing to stop us bringing in the bulldozers the next day and levelling the place. And, what's more, you would make a handsome profit from the wedding gift. All right, I know that once you marry her then half of everything you own will be hers, but you could get around that with a pre-nuptial. My solicitor is red-hot on things like that.'

Ray swore lightly under his breath. 'That is the most preposterous thing I have ever heard. And what makes you think Caitlin would want to go along with a crazy scheme like that?'

'Come on, Ray, you could sweet-talk her around if you really wanted to.'

'This is Caitlin we are talking about,' Ray reminded him. 'She loves the house and doesn't want to sell it…and what is more she is probably still in love with her ex-fiancé.'

'Great, so catch her on the rebound,' Philippe said jovially. 'This makes good business sense for both of you. I know you like her, Ray. I saw the way you looked at her when we all had dinner that night. And you've obviously taken her to bed.'

'That is none of your damn business, Philippe,' Ray cut across him furiously.

'Look, all I'm saying is consider it. As I see it you've got nothing to lose and everything to gain; a beautiful woman in your bed and a healthy profit. And if you don't like being married to her you can always divorce her and it probably won't cost you as much as losing out on this land deal—'

'You know something, Philippe,' Ray cut across him heavily. 'You've got a disgustingly mercenary mind.'

Far from being outraged, Philippe laughed. 'Just think about it, that's all I am saying.

Anyhow, have you received that copy of Murdo's will that I faxed you earlier?'

'Yes, it is here on my desk, but I'm not interested, Philippe, and you are going too far.' Ray's voice was tight with anger.

'Well, you should at least look at it. And I don't wish to be too intrusive or mercenary, Ray, but remember these were Murdo's last wishes and should be respected. Anyway, I'll talk to you Monday... Oh, and by the way, Sadie thought the idea was great. She said it was about time you took the matrimonial plunge again, even if it is only for six months.'

Ray put the phone down in disgust. Then he sat still for a moment, Philippe's words thumping through his mind, before pushing his chair back and going in search of Caitlin.

He found her outside on the patio; she was leaning against the wrought-iron railing looking down at the street below.

'Everything okay?' She turned and looked at him as he came to stand next to her and she was surprised to see a glitter of anger in his eyes.

'Yes, everything is just fine.'

It didn't sound as if it was, but she didn't press him. Instead she said gently, 'You know, I think you are right about throwing yourself into work. It does help take your mind off things. I feel a lot better when I'm busy.'

His eyes moved over her contemplatively. The breeze was ruffling her hair back from her face. She had a beautiful bone structure, high cheekbones, perfectly proportioned lips that were full and sensuous, a small button nose and eyes that shimmered with beauty. All in all she was a very desirable package.

Aware that he seemed to be watching her very closely, she felt her heart start to speed up with a mixture of desire and uncertainty. Desperately she sought to keep her mind away from the longing he could fire up in her. 'And I've been giving Murdo's house a bit of thought,' she said.

'Well, it is your favourite subject.'

Caitlin decided it was best to ignore the wry comment and continued swiftly. 'I was wondering if I should take the wall down between the dining room and the lounge and put in an archway. What do you think?'

There was a flicker of amusement in his gaze now. 'Why are you asking me?'

'Because you are an architect and I wanted a professional opinion,' she said, a small frown playing between her eyes.

'Well, you know what I think,' he said softly. 'I think the place should be demolished.'

'Ray, that is not funny.' She put one hand on her hip and glared at him. 'That is Murdo's house you are talking about!'

'It's your house,' he corrected her softly. 'To do with as you see fit.'

'Yes, and I see fit to restore it lovingly to its former glory.'

'I know.' Ray put one hand under her chin, tipping her face so that she was forced to meet his gaze. 'Tell me, Caitlin, did you ever see Murdo's will?' He watched her face, searching for any flicker of emotion that might tell him she knew the terms Murdo had laid down.

Caitlin frowned, the question taking her very much by surprise. 'Well, no…of course not. I got a letter from the solicitor telling me of my inheritance. And I saw him briefly in his office to collect the keys. But I didn't actually see the will.' She shrugged. 'Why? Should I have done?'

'No. I just wondered what you knew about the conditions of sale, that's all.'

'All he said was that I've got to live there for six months before I can sell it. And he told me that there were a few special conditions attached to the will regarding that. I didn't pay much attention to that part of things, to be honest, because I was just so thrilled to be inheriting a house, selling it was the last thing on my mind. Oh, and he told me to get back in touch with him if my marital status was going to change.' She grimaced slightly. 'I told him there was no chance of that.'

Ray nodded. It was quite clear to him that Caitlin had no inkling of Murdo's final wishes.

'Why are you asking, anyway?' She looked up at him, puzzled by the questions. 'You are not still obsessed with buying the place, are you, Ray? I thought we'd agreed to forget that.'

'You were the one who brought up the subject of the house,' he reminded her with a grin.

'Yes, well, I'm sorry I did now. That joke about bulldozing the place wasn't funny.'

He smiled and leaned a little closer. 'Caitlin,' he said softly, 'it's just a house, let's forget it and move on to more interesting subjects.'

'Like what?' she asked breathlessly as his lips hovered a fraction from hers.

'Like this, of course...' And then he kissed her with deeply searing, purposeful kisses. And suddenly Caitlin forgot all about the house...all about Ray's love for Hélène...and all about David.

CHAPTER NINE

IT WAS early Sunday morning. Caitlin cuddled closer to Ray in the deep comfort of the double bed and listened to the sound of church bells drifting on the air. She wished that time would stand still and they could lie entwined in each other's arms like this forever. But unfortunately their flight home was at twelve-thirty this afternoon...so time was running out.

She glanced up at Ray, studying the lean, handsome features as he slept. His lashes were dark and thick against his cheek. He had eyelashes that any woman would be proud of, she thought hazily, and his mouth was softly sensuous. Remembering the heat of his kisses last night made her go hot all over and stirred a feeling of renewed need inside her. She stretched up and kissed him softly on his lips. His arms tightened around her waist and he returned the kiss sleepily, his eyes flicking open.

'Mmm, that is a nice way to wake up,' he murmured lazily.

'I was just thinking the same myself.' She rolled over and leaned against his chest, looking down at him with a smile. This close, his eyes were a gorgeous shade of deep molasses honey.

He reached up and stroked his hands through her hair, then, cupping her face, he kissed her tenderly.

The phone cut through the silence of the morning.

Caitlin groaned and wound her arms around his neck. 'Does your phone never stop ringing? Just ignore it,' she murmured.

Ray continued to kiss her back and she thought he was going to do just that, but then suddenly he was pulling away from her. 'I've just remembered that Philippe said he'd phone me this morning,' he said, sliding out from under her.

Caitlin watched with disappointment as he walked away from her to pick up his robe from the chair. She had a brief glimpse of his powerful body before he had put the robe on and disappeared out of the bedroom door.

Caitlin wished he wasn't able to switch quite so easily from thinking about passion to business. It sent a small feeling of disquiet through her. Surely he could have let the answer machine take that call? After all, it was Sunday morning.

With a sigh she climbed out of bed and reached for her dressing gown. She was being selfish, she told herself firmly. Trouble was, she couldn't seem to help herself.

Tying the belt of her gown firmly around her waist, she walked through to the kitchen and put the kettle on.

'Bad news, I'm afraid,' Ray said as he joined her a few moments later. 'I'm not going to be able to fly back to Provence with you today. That was Philippe and some problems have cropped up that I'm going to have to take care of at the office. I'll drop you out at the airport first, though.'

'There is no need, Ray,' she said quickly. 'I can take a taxi to the airport.'

'Always so independent,' he mocked her lightly, and then as she made to move away from him he caught hold of her hand and pulled her back. 'Okay, but I'll only allow you to take a taxi to the airport if you will have dinner with me on Wednesday night?'

She pretended to think about it for a moment. 'All right, you've got a deal, but come over to my place and I'll cook for you.'

'Sounds wonderful.' He pressed a kiss against her lips. 'You can impress me with your *cuisine anglaise,*' he murmured teasingly.

She smiled up into his eyes. 'And you can impress me with your architectural skills and give me your opinion on that wall that I'm thinking of taking out...'

'I thought you wanted to cook for me and all along you've got an ulterior motive.' He shook his head. 'I can see I've met my match with you, Caitlin Palmer.'

'You've caught me red-handed,' she said with a smile.

He kissed her softly on the lips again. 'Wednesday it is, then,' he said gently as he moved back. 'Now I've got to shower and leave you, I'm afraid, but I'll ring that taxi for you before I go.'

It seemed strange being left alone in Ray's apartment. Caitlin showered and changed and packed up her bag. Then she wandered around and tidied up while she waited for the taxi. Her steps led her into the office and she collected the champagne glass Ray had left on the desk last night. As she did her glance fell on the papers neatly stacked by the phone and Murdo's name caught her attention.

She moved the papers slightly and they slid down onto the floor. Hastily she bent to pick them up and that was when she realised that what she was looking at was a copy of Murdo's last will and testament.

Caitlin frowned as she remembered the way Ray had questioned her last night about Murdo's will. Why had he questioned her about it when he already had a copy? Why did he even have a copy? The answer to that was easy: *he hadn't given up on buying her house.*

Frowning, she leafed through the papers. Pinned to the will there was a note from Philippe. It was in French and she had difficulty in understanding it...something about marriage being a solution, which didn't make any sense. Caitlin sat down in Ray's chair and leafed further through the papers. There were some plans folded at the back and she spread them out across the desk. At first she didn't know what she was looking at, then she realised that Ray's château was marked on the map, and Murdo's house and behind it several other houses.

But there were no other houses behind Murdo's. She frowned and flicked back to the note Philippe had sent, and wished her French were better. Why was marriage the solution...and a solution to what?

The sound of the front door slamming made her jump nervously.

'Hi, Caitlin, it is only me,' Ray's voice called out from the lounge. 'I forgot some documents that I need.'

For a second Caitlin thought about hurriedly putting the papers away so as not to be caught snooping, but then she dismissed the notion. This concerned her land and she needed to know what was going on.

'Caitlin...' His voice trailed off as he reached the office door and saw her sitting behind his desk. 'What are you up to?' he asked warily as he noticed the papers spread out in front of her.

'I was just about to ask you the same question.' Her voice was brittle.

He came further into the room. 'The papers you are rooting through are private,' he said, an edge of annoyance creeping into his tone.

'But they concern me, don't they, Ray?' Her heart started to thump with painful rapid strokes, but it wasn't with anger, it was with cold dread. The mood between them earlier had been so playful and tender. She remembered the way they had actually teased each other about having ulterior motives...and now suspicion and distrust were twisting everything inside her. 'You led me to believe that you wanted my property because it was a minor inconvenience having to drive across it towards one of your many entrances. But that wasn't the truth, was it?' Her eyes drifted to the plans lying by Murdo's will. 'I'm blocking more than an entrance to your house, aren't I?' Her voice was icy with realisation. 'In fact I'm obviously a major headache...that's why you've gone to so much trouble getting a copy of Murdo's will so you could find out how to get rid of me before the six months were up...that's probably why you've invited me here...' As everything tumbled into place her eyes darkened with pain. 'And it's probably why you've taken me to bed—'

'Caitlin, that isn't true,' he cut across her quietly. 'I invited you here because I wanted to spend time with you—'

'Just cut out the smooth talk, Ray, because it's not going to wash with me,' she intercepted him fiercely. 'I'm not stupid—I can see exactly what has been going on here.' She flicked the paper on the desk contemptuously. 'I knew there would never be anything deep and meaningful between us. But I never thought that you would stoop to this.'

'Caitlin if you would just listen for a moment—'

'I don't want to listen to anything you say ever again.' Her eyes blazed with fury now. 'And don't flatter yourself that you can get round me with platitudes, because, to be honest, going to bed with you was a light-hearted fling, something to take my mind away from the real love of my life.' As she said the words she noticed how his eyes narrowed on her and she hoped vehemently that she had struck a blow to his arrogant male ego. But also at the same time something twisted inside her painfully, and she knew that her words were anything but honest. Sleeping with Ray had meant so much more than that. 'But I thought we were at least truthful with each other,' she finished huskily.

'I have never made any secret of the fact that I wanted to buy your land.' Ray's voice was terse now.

'But you didn't tell me about this.' Furiously she swept the papers off the desk and onto the floor.

'I didn't tell you because I didn't think it would help matters.'

'Well, you were right there, because the answer to your offer is still no.' She stood up. 'And what the hell is this marriage solution that Philippe has written about?'

'You have been digging, haven't you?' Ray said calmly.

'What is it, Ray?' she asked again, fixing him with a rigid stare.

He bent and retrieved the papers to put them back on the desk. 'Apparently the only way around the six-months stipulation for selling is if you and I marry.' He watched as her skin blanched, then went on tersely. 'Apparently

Murdo specified that if we marry the house will be mine and, what is more, he has placed a large amount of money in a trust fund somewhere as a wedding present for us.'

'So what were you planning, Ray—a whirlwind romance and wedding followed by a lightning divorce?' Her heart was thundering so hard against her chest that it felt tight with pain. 'I hope you were planning to get down on one knee when you ask me,' she added darkly. 'That way it will feel so much more satisfying when I say no.'

His lips twisted in a mirthless smile. 'I think you are getting a little ahead of the game, Caitlin,' he said coolly. 'Because I haven't asked you to marry me.'

'Saving that for a cosy night in with me on Wednesday?' She tossed her hair back from her face as she marched past him. 'Well, you can go to hell, Ray. I'd rather marry the devil incarnate than take any vow with you.'

She had almost reached the door when he caught hold of her arm. 'Just hold it right there,' he said angrily and swung her around to face him. 'Just for the record, it was Philippe who came up with the marriage suggestion and I told him to go to hell. And I didn't tell you about the land development because I didn't want to put that much pressure on you to leave. And thirdly I invited you here for purely personal reasons.'

Caitlin swallowed hard. She wanted so much to believe him...but she just couldn't.

The sound of the doorbell cut through the silence.

'That will be my taxi.' With a supreme effort of will she pulled away from him.

Ray followed her out into the lounge and watched as she picked up her bag from behind the door.

'Caitlin, you are making a big mistake,' he said quietly.

'I don't think so.'

'The fact is that I could have had you out of that house quicker than you think.'

The arrogant confidence of his tone made her pause with her hand on the door handle. 'The house is mine, Ray—' she glanced around at him angrily '—and there is nothing you can do about that.'

'I think there is. Go back to your house and find out where your water supply comes from.'

'What the hell are you talking about?' Caitlin frowned. 'I know I'm not connected to the mains, if that's what you mean, but I've got my own well.'

He shook his head. 'Correction, you've got *my* well. You see, I could have cut you off from your only supply of water ages ago. I just chose not to because it seemed like a very unpleasant thing to do. I preferred the gentle approach. But...' he shrugged '...if you want to take the gloves off and play rough, then fair enough. It's your choice.'

Caitlin stared at him. 'Are you threatening me?'

'No. I'm telling you a point of fact. Any water you have comes courtesy of me. Go back and check it out.' He shrugged. 'Then when you've come to your senses and you realise that I am trying to play fair with you, we'll talk.'

'I don't want to talk to you ever again,' Caitlin said furiously. She turned and opened the door. 'Cut the water off if it makes you feel better.' She tossed the words back at him over her shoulder. 'It won't get you anywhere.'

Then she closed the door behind her, gently but very firmly.

All the way to the airport Caitlin's blood boiled with anger. She was seething with Ray and she was furious with herself for having ever gone to bed with him. How could she have been so stupid? Why hadn't she realised what he was up to?

She reran conversations in her head, searching through for the signs that she had missed. And she remembered especially how he had hesitated when she had asked him directly if there were any hard feelings about her not selling to him. How he had looked amused by her passion for Murdo's house. What was it he had said? 'Some advice, Caitlin… Never fall in love with a business project. You should be objective and unemotional at all times.'

Those words burnt through her mind now and she felt stupid and used and cheap. She had obviously been the business project and he had wined and dined her and probably taken her to bed with only one purpose in mind.

The pain that knowledge caused her was unbelievable. She kept telling herself that she didn't care, that she had no feelings for him anyway. That it had just been a light-hearted fling on her part. But the words were hollow inside her. And the pain just wouldn't subside.

CHAPTER TEN

THE sun rose over the mountains and slanted through the olive grove in a yellow misty haze. Somewhere a cockerel crowed its distinctive notes clear on the silent early morning air. But Caitlin was already awake. She hadn't been sleeping well since her return from Paris and that was a week ago now. Despite the fact that she felt lethargic, she threw the covers of the bed back and went into the kitchen to turn on the tap.

It had become a daily routine. The first thing she did every morning was check the water and she did the same again at regular intervals throughout the day, and sometimes she even got up in the middle of the night just to turn on the tap to check it again. Each time after a few seconds' delay cool water gushed freely and it was the same this morning, a few tense seconds waiting, then water flowed with forceful pressure into the sink. Hastily Caitlin put the kettle under the tap so as not to waste a precious drop. Then she set the kettle on the stove and opened the back door.

It was a glorious morning; the sun was milky warm against her skin and a little bird sat in one of the branches of an almond tree and sang joyously as if life was full of promise. But life wouldn't be full of promise around here if Ray got his way, Caitlin thought darkly. The olive grove would be demolished along with the house and there would be no almond tree for the little bird to sing in. She bit down on her lip and tried not to think about it. Ray was a monster, she told herself sharply, an absolute monster.

So why hadn't he cut the water off? That was the question that plagued her most these days. As soon as she had returned to the house she had lost no time investigating his claims that the well was on his land, and she had found that he was telling the truth. The well lay half a mile inside his boundary. This meant he could have cut her off ages ago. And yet he had chosen not to.

Obviously he had decided that it wouldn't do him any good, she told herself firmly. And he was right, it wouldn't, because no matter what he did she wasn't going to give in and sell. She had already made provisions for the water crisis. All the buckets and the bath had been filled and she had ordered a water tank that should arrive some time next week. As soon as that was installed and filled it would give her some breathing space. She wasn't going to go down without a fight.

But the fact that she should have to fight Ray still astonished and hurt her. She couldn't believe how calculating he had been. Especially when she remembered how passionately he had kissed her and held her. When she lay in bed at night she squeezed her eyes shut and tried to forget how good it had felt to be in his arms. But the memories were hard to erase.

The really strange thing was that she had thought her breakup from David had hurt, but it was nothing to the torment inside her now.

'You are really very bad when it comes to choosing men, Caitlin,' she told herself angrily. 'You'd be better advised to give them up totally. Join a nunnery.'

The shrill whistle of the kettle made her return to the kitchen. As she made herself some ground coffee she tried to switch her mind away from Ray and think instead about the day ahead. There was a local market on in the village today and she wanted to go down and buy some fresh vegetables and provisions.

She turned the immersion on so that she could have a shower. Then she sat at the kitchen table and sipped her coffee as she made a shopping list. She had just finished when the phone rang and she picked it up expecting it to be her mother or Heidi.

Instead it was Ray's lazily relaxed tone that echoed down the line. 'Hi. Are you ready to talk yet?' he inquired, and instantly every nerve inside her seemed to tense.

'I'm surprised you've got the nerve to phone me.' She felt strangely breathless as she spoke, her emotions twisting inside her as if she were pulling them through a wringer. But the really dreadful part was the weakness inside her that was glad to hear his voice; she fought against that furiously. 'And, no, I am not ready to talk to you and I never will be.'

'Come on, Caitlin, this is silly,' he said impatiently. 'I've given you a whole week to cool off and think about things and that's long enough. Now I think we should meet up and talk about this like civilised adults.'

His tone grated on her. How dared he talk to her as if she were some recalcitrant child? 'Just go to hell.'

'What are you doing today?' he asked as if she hadn't spoken.

'I'm going down to the market to do some shopping, not that it is any of your damn business.' She frowned and wondered what on earth had possessed her to even tell him that. 'Look, I never want to see you again, Ray,' she continued swiftly. 'And I'm going to hang up now. So goodbye.' She disconnected him and sat drumming her fingers against the table, trying to gather her senses. How did he manage to churn her up so easily? Just the sound of his voice made her literally go weak at the knees and it really irritated her.

Hastily she got to her feet and went to have her shower. She wasn't going to give Ray one more thought. Not one.

Why was it, she wondered a few minutes later as she stood under the forceful jet of water from the shower, that every man in her life had let her down? It had started with her father, he had walked out of her life when she was twelve and she hadn't seen him for five years. Then there had been Julian, who had said all the right things but been as insincere as hell—then David—and now there was Ray to add to the list. And it was strange because, of all the betrayals, Ray was the one that hurt the most. She felt kind of numb inside. It was inexplicable because she hadn't known him that long. But the memory of his kisses, his caresses, his whispered words of passion were emblazed on her mind along with the way he sometimes looked at her, with that quizzical intensity, that tender gleam of humour...just thinking about it now made her insides wrench with longing.

She raised her head to the jet of water and fiercely tried not to think about him. And that was when the water flicked off.

At first she thought that she had leant back against the switch and then it dawned on her: she hadn't switched it off, she had been cut off.

With shaking hands she reached for a towel and wrapped it around her. And just to check that it wasn't the shower that was faulty, she walked over to the sink and turned the tap on. Nothing happened.

Caitlin was furious; she could hardly believe that Ray had actually stooped so low. Then she reminded herself that this was the man who had cold-bloodedly set out to seduce her to win her around to his way of thinking. Of course he would stoop that low.

Her mobile phone rang and she snatched it up.

'Have I got your attention now?' Ray asked coolly.

'I won't be bullied into submission, Ray.' To her dismay her voice shook slightly.

'All I'm asking is that you meet me down in the village for lunch,' he continued as if she hadn't spoken. 'You told me you were going down there anyway, so it's hardly out of your way.'

'I don't want to meet you for lunch,' she said stonily.

'Do you want your water back on?'

'You know I do.' Her voice was tightly controlled now.

'Okay, so repeat after me. Yes, I will meet you for lunch at one-thirty at the restaurant in the main village square.'

Go to hell, were the words Caitlin wanted to say. She was silent for a long moment as she tried to think rationally. Cold water dripped down her face and her back from her wet hair and the hand that held her mobile was tight. She wanted to hang up or tell him she had made contingency plans and she would get through this. But then she found herself backing down. 'All right, I'll meet you.' Maybe she should talk to him, she told herself firmly. If only to tell him to his face what she thought of him. 'But just for a coffee,' she added hastily. 'I couldn't eat lunch—it would choke me.'

'Always so dramatic,' he said, a hint of amusement in his tone now. 'I'll see you later, Caitlin.'

A few minutes later the water started to run in the shower again.

An hour later Caitlin was driving down the narrow country roads towards the village.

She was going to tell Ray exactly what she thought of him, she told herself all the way down and around the hairpin bends. There was no way she would ever back down now.

Caitlin parked her car on the outskirts of the village under the shade of some trees and glanced at her watch. She had an hour to kill before their meeting. Trying to ignore the little prickles of apprehension that burst inside her, she found her shopping list, and taking her bag, stepped out of the car.

The village of Ezure was perched on the side of the mountain and was picture-postcard perfect. Shady lanes with cobbled surfaces wound steeply down past quaint old houses before finally opening out into a wide tree-lined square.

Although the community was only thirty miles from the tourism of the coast it was completely unspoilt; there was an air almost of stepping back in time about it. There were only a few shops, a couple of restaurants and one bar. And when Caitlin had ventured down during the week the place had been virtually deserted; the only sound had been the gurgle of water from the fountains and the soft thud of boules as some elderly men had played the traditional game under the shade of the giant eucalyptus trees.

Today, however, the village seemed to have awoken from its dreamlike trance and it rang with the sound of children laughing, and people talking. As she rounded the corner into the square she found it was alive with the colourful, vibrant buzz of the local market. The stalls were covered in wide awnings that created a shady place to shop, but even so the heat was intense and Caitlin was glad she had put on a lightweight summer dress as she pressed through the crowd to wander along the stalls.

There were mountains of juicy black and green olives and a range of fresh vegetables that looked as if they had just been pulled fresh from local gardens, goats' cheese and fresh preserves and a mouth-watering array of freshly baked bread. The smell of cooked chickens mingled with the scent of fresh herbs and ground coffee in a way that was somehow uniquely French. Caitlin enjoyed browsing along the lines of wares. She bought some ingredients for a salad and was queuing up to buy some crusty bread when suddenly she didn't feel very well.

The wave of dizziness and nausea hit her from nowhere and hastily she turned and left the stall, her one thought to get to somewhere cool and sit down quickly before she fell down.

It was a relief when she emerged into the open space at the other side of the square. There were views across the rolling countryside towards the sea from here and a soft breeze blew in that helped quell the sick feeling. She sat down on the wall under the shade of one of the eucalyptus trees and closed her eyes for a moment.

'Caitlin.' Ray's voice instantly made her alert and she looked up quickly.

'I thought it was you,' he said as he strolled across towards her. 'I saw you hurrying out of the market...' He trailed off suddenly and his eyes raked over the pallor of her skin with a look of concern. 'Are you okay? You look terrible.'

'Thanks.' Her voice was dry.

'No, I mean it. You really don't look well.' He sat down beside her on the wall and reached to put a hand on her forehead.

The touch of his skin so cool against the heat of hers sent a million different reactions spinning through her, and amidst the confusion the one overriding emotion was the weakness of longing. She flinched away from him appalled by such a pathetic reaction. This was

the man who had used her for purely mercenary reasons, she reminded herself fiercely.
And maybe he did sound concerned but all he
really cared about was his land and his business. 'I'm fine, Ray, don't fuss. The heat just
got to me for a moment, that's all.'

He dropped his hand back down to his side.
'Are you drinking enough water?' he asked.
'Because in these temperatures it's very easy
to dehydrate.'

'Coming from the man who cut my supply
this morning, that is a bit of a joke, isn't it?'
She glared up at him.

'You should be drinking bottled water, not
the stuff that comes from your tap,' he reminded her quickly. 'And I cut the supply for
five minutes, Caitlin, so let's not exaggerate
this.'

'It was still a lousy thing to do,' she said
furiously. 'How did you manage to do that
anyhow?'

'The connections have been set up like that
for easy maintenance and I have control over
them.'

'Well, I won't forgive you for it.'

For a moment his eyes moved over her face contemplatively. The colour had returned to her cheeks and her eyes glistened with vivid green fires of passion.

'It got your attention, though, didn't it?' he said softly. 'And I wanted to see you.'

The words and the way he looked at her made her emotions dip dizzily. Confused, she looked away.

'I've missed you this week,' he continued softly.

She looked up at him then and her heart lurched crazily. The truth was that she had missed him as well, missed him more than she could ever have believed possible.

There was no doubt about it; there was a powerful chemistry between them. It was uncurling now in waves that seemed even more forceful than the sun. But it didn't mean anything, she told herself furiously. And his words were insincere. All he cared about was her land.

The strong reminder gave her the courage to shake her head. 'Well, I haven't missed you,' she said huskily. As she made to look away again he reached out and caught hold of her face, forcing her to hold his gaze.

'I've thought about you every day and every night.'

The whispered words sent her emotions into total chaos.

Her eyes moved to his lips and she found herself remembering how wonderful they felt against hers, how easily he could stir up a wild, uncontrolled passion that she hadn't even known existed inside her until the day he'd taken her into his arms. *She loved him.* The knowledge sneaked unbidden into her subconscious and it shocked her so much that she felt dizzy with fear.

Ray watched as her skin drained of all colour and his hand dropped from her skin, his eyes narrowed. 'Caitlin?'

Released from the touch of his hand, she lost no time in moving away. 'Look, I shouldn't have agreed to meet you,' she said breathlessly. 'You can throw as many compliments and soft words at me as you like but it won't make me change my mind. I've got your measure, Ray, and—'

As she made to stand up he caught hold of her arm, forcing her to sit.

'The little exercise with your water this morning was to show you that if I'd wanted you out of that house and off that land I could have made life much more difficult for you ages ago. But I haven't.'

'Only because you knew it wouldn't work.' Her heart was slamming fiercely against her chest. And she wanted to put her hands over her ears like a child and block out his words.

'I've also pulled a few strings to get your electricity supply restored quickly.' His eyes hardened on her. 'Do you think I would have done that if I'd wanted you gone?'

'Stop it, Ray.' She tried to pull away from him but still he wouldn't release her. 'I don't want to hear any more of your lies. You are just a user and—'

'I know you've been hurt in the past, Caitlin.' He said the words softly. 'I can see it in your eyes sometimes when you look at me. But I'm not David…and I'm not anyone who is going to use you, or hurt you, or deceive you…because I love you.'

For a heart-stopping moment Caitlin thought she had misheard him. She stopped struggling to escape from him and then he let her go.

'I asked you to come to Paris with me because I wanted *you*. There were no ulterior motives concerning your property...no shady deals...just a desire to be with you and hold you in my arms.'

Caitlin stared up at him wordlessly. She wanted so much to believe him.

'From the first moment when you opened the door to me at Murdo's house I felt drawn to you. You blew me away Caitlin. It was like...' He trailed off for a moment.

'What was it like?' she asked him huskily, her eyes wide with puzzlement and bewilderment.

'It was like history repeating itself,' he said softly. Then he reached out and stroked her hair back from her face with a tender caress. 'It was the same way I'd felt about Hélène, and it was an emotion I didn't think I would ever experience again... It scared me.'

The husky timbre of his voice startled her. Ray was so powerfully controlled and always so confident. To hear him say he'd been scared by anything astonished her.

'I found myself making up all kinds of excuses to keep myself away from you. Told myself that you were probably just a gold-digger, that you had fooled Murdo into thinking you were a decent, caring person. And then you arrived...' He trailed off. 'And I found myself running out of excuses to keep away from you, because you are decent and caring and wonderful. In fact you are everything I love.'

She didn't say anything for a long moment. Her heart was thundering so loudly that it was deafening her. 'You're just saying this.' Her voice felt stiff. She wanted so much to believe him, but she was really scared now. How did she know that she could trust him? He could hurt her so badly and she didn't think she could bear it... 'Look. I've got to go.' She stood up abruptly.

'Caitlin...'

She was aware that he called out after her but she didn't look back.

CHAPTER ELEVEN

AS CAITLIN made her way through the crowds Ray's words pounded through her brain. 'I'm not David…and I'm not anyone who is going to use you, or hurt you, or deceive you… because I love you.'

She wanted so much to believe him, but she couldn't allow herself to. 'You are a sensible and mature woman, Caitlin Palmer,' she told herself firmly. 'You know very well that Ray has everything to gain by sweet-talking his way around you, and nothing to lose. *You can't trust him.*'

She repeated the mantra over and over again until she reached the safety of her car. Once inside she took a few moments to compose herself before starting the engine. She had done the right thing walking away from him, she told herself firmly. There was no way she was going to leave herself wide open to being hurt again. She'd been there and got the T-shirt. Only a fool went back for more.

What about the fact that you've fallen in love with him? a little voice whispered inside her, cutting through all the strong, angry words with a force that was overwhelming. She tried desperately to close it out. Of course she didn't love him—that was ridiculous, absolutely ridiculous. But even as she denied the words she was remembering again the way Ray had looked at her, the things he had said—*'I've thought about you every day and every night.'*—and her heart was turning over with a raw need to believe him because she loved him so much. She had thought of him every day and every night as well and the thought of being without him was the worst feeling ever. It was as if someone had blown a great big hole inside her and the vast gap would never, ever be filled.

How was she going to go on without him? How was she going to cope with this raw ache inside her? Her eyes misted with tears and fiercely she brushed them away. She had coped before and she would cope now. Angrily she put the car in reverse and looked behind her. A car pulled up, blocking her way, and she waited patiently for a few minutes for it to move. But it didn't move and as she watched in her mirror the driver's door opened and someone stepped out.

And that was when she realised it was Ray and her heart started to thunder wildly against her chest.

Taking a deep breath, she wound her window down. 'Will you please move your car? You are in my way.' She was amazed by how cool and composed she sounded.

'I'm not going anywhere, Caitlin, because we haven't finished our conversation.' He sounded just as coolly composed.

Caitlin watched in the mirror as he came closer and hurriedly she pushed the button that would lock all her doors. 'I've said all I've got to say, Ray. So please go.' She gripped the driving wheel with tense hands and didn't dare glance sideways at him as he crouched down beside the door.

'I'm not going, Caitlin. So you may as well get out of the car and talk to me.'

'If you don't move your car I'll make a scene,' she warned him shakily.

'Will you?' She could hear a faint edge of amusement in his tone now. 'What are you going to do?'

Angrily she leaned on her car horn and the sound reverberated loudly down the empty street. 'There, that is what I will do.' She took her hand off the horn and glared at him through the open window. 'And I'm going to keep doing it until you move.'

His lips twisted in a roguishly amused smile. 'Well, go ahead. I wouldn't mind an audience anyway. A few witnesses might come in handy.'

'A few witnesses for what?' she asked warily.

He held up a sheaf of papers. 'These are the legal papers for the land deal with Philippe.'

Caitlin bit down on her lip. 'I don't care what they are, Ray, I just want you to move your car so that I can go home.' She leaned her hand on the horn again and a few people started to gather on the pavement behind them.

Ray ignored the noise and the people completely as he held the papers for her to see. 'Look at them,' he demanded, pushing them further in front of her face so that she had no alternative but to see they were the same papers that had lain on his desk in Paris. Then slowly he started to tear them up with forceful, positive strokes.

Caitlin's hand fell away from the horn as she watched pieces of papers fluttering down beside her in jagged chunks.

'This is what I think about the land deal with Philippe,' he said steadily. 'Listen to me, Caitlin. I love you and there are going to be no *gîtes,* the deal is off.'

She didn't answer him immediately; her heart was thundering so loudly against her chest that she could hardly hear herself think.

Ray allowed the rest of the papers to fall onto her lap. Then he turned to the few people who were watching with interest. 'I'm in love with this woman,' he said loudly in French. 'And I want the whole world to know it.' There was a ripple of applause and a few whistles of encouragement as a few more people rounded the corner to listen. 'And I want everyone to know that there will be no *gîtes* built anywhere near her land, because the last thing in the world I would ever want would be to hurt her.'

'Ray, will you stop it?' Caitlin murmured as there was another round of applause. 'You're making a scene.'

'I thought that was what you wanted,' he said, looking back at her.

As she looked up at him her eyes blurred with tears and a drop rolled down her cheeks and landed on the paper. 'I don't know what I want,' she admitted huskily. 'All I know is that I don't want to be hurt again, Ray. I…couldn't bear it…'

'Just unlock the door, Caitlin, and get out of the car,' he said gently.

After a moment's hesitation she did as he asked and paper fluttered down around their feet like confetti as she stepped outside.

She stood and looked up at him and he reached out and wiped the tears from under her eyes with tender fingers. 'I'm so sorry, Caitlin,' he whispered gently. 'I never wanted to make you cry and I never wanted to hurt you. But what I said to you before is the whole truth…I invited you to Paris because I wanted *you;* there was no other reason—and no ulterior motives. I promise you that, sincerely.'

There was no doubting the honesty of his tone and suddenly all her defences came tumbling down around her. She believed him but couldn't find her voice to answer him; it seemed choked under a weight of emotion that was far too heavy for her.

'All I'm asking is that you give me a chance to prove myself to you,' he said, his voice earnest and pleading. 'I know you still love David. I know this is all too soon for you but I'm prepared to wait for you, Caitlin. I'll wait for as long as it takes.'

'Philippe is not going to be pleased.' She managed the words hoarsely.

'To hell with Philippe,' Ray said sweepingly. 'And meanwhile I've organised contractors to come out and connect your property to the main water supply. They should be with you tomorrow.'

'And you are doing all this for me?' she whispered huskily.

'I'd do anything for you, Caitlin,' he said seriously. 'And anyway I've decided you are right—Murdo's house is full of character and potential. A person would have to be mad to knock it down.'

She looked up at him and suddenly she started to laugh and at the same time another tear trickled down her cheek. 'I never thought I'd hear you say something like that.'

'And after Hélène I never thought I would fall in love again.'

The gentle words caused more tears to stream down her cheeks.

'Don't cry, my love.' He reached out to wipe her tears away with a soothing hand. And the next moment she was being cradled in his arms. 'I never wanted to hurt you,' he whispered fiercely. 'I admit, when you first got here, I told myself that my priority was to get you out and get the land. But the idea started to crumble within an hour of being in your company. From time to time I tried to rekindle it, told myself I was a businessman first and foremost, and then you'd look at me with those adorable green eyes and honestly I couldn't have cared less about business…'

'I can hardly believe you are saying all this,' she whispered breathlessly. 'I keep wondering if I'm dreaming—'

She pulled back. 'And if it's a dream it is the most wonderful one.' Caitlin looked into his eyes and she felt her insides melt with the heat of desire and suddenly she was reaching up to kiss him.

For a long moment they were wrapped in each other's arms, their kisses growing more and more heated and passionate. It was only as they became aware of the cheers and applause from the crowd gathered behind them that Ray pulled back from her. 'Let's get out of here,' he said softly.

Wordlessly she allowed him to lead her back to his car. She slipped into the passenger seat and then watched as he locked her car before getting in beside her and driving slowly up through the winding narrow streets.

'I should really have driven my own car home,' she murmured, trying to think sensibly as they rounded a corner away from it.

'I'll get someone to pick it up for you later,' he said as he continued on until they were out into the countryside. 'You aren't in any fit state to drive anyway.' He slanted a glance across at her and watched as she found a tissue and dabbed at her eyes. 'How are you feeling now?'

'Shell-shocked,' she admitted wryly. 'I was so hurt and angry when I drove down here this morning, I can hardly take in what you have said.'

'But it is the truth,' he said softly.

The car rounded a corner and Murdo's house came into view.

'We are friends again, aren't we?' he asked as he pulled the car to a halt by the front door.

She didn't answer him immediately.

'Caitlin?' He looked over at her anxiously.

'I thought we were a little more than friends,' she whispered softly. 'Didn't you say something about being in love with me?' She slanted a shy look across at him. 'Did you say you'd wait for me?'

He gave that lopsided smile that she knew so well. 'I love you with all of my heart and I'll wait for you until the end of time.'

She swallowed on a deep knot of emotion. 'And I love you,' she whispered unsteadily. 'With all my heart.'

For a moment there was a deep silence as he stared at her, his dark eyes intense, a muscle flexed in his cheek.

'I...I thought that maybe the deep feelings I was experiencing with you meant that I was on the rebound,' she continued, her voice so low it was barely audible. 'But the truth of the matter is I've never felt this way about anyone before. In fact I realise now that I was never truly in love with David, whereas with you it's the real thing. I adore you, Ray, and I'd do anything for you...' She shrugged hopelessly. 'So if you are stringing me a line...you know about the house...' a tear trickled down her cheek. '...well, you don't have to. You can have the property because right at this moment it is singularly unimportant.'

'Caitlin.' He reached and folded her into his arms. 'I want *you* and nothing else matters, so please get that into your mind.' His lips found hers and he kissed her with the hungry passion that she had been craving all through these long, lonely nights apart from him.

'God, I love you so much...' She wound her arms up and around his neck. For a long time they just kissed, their caresses filled with the anguish and relief of a love that knew no bounds.

'Shall we go inside?' she whispered tremulously as his hands grew more passionately insistent and her body cried out for so much more.

He smiled. 'Where is the young woman who practically ran from me the last time I drove her home?'

The return of that teasing humour in his eyes made her smile.

'She's given in to a power much stronger than herself...' she whispered.

Ray reached for the door handle and they climbed out into the sunshine. He waited for her to come around and join him, then he held out his hand and took hold of her.

'Caitlin, before we go inside I've got something to ask you,' he said solemnly.

She looked up at him. 'What is it?' she asked nervously.

Then suddenly he got down on one knee by the front door of the property.

'Caitlin, will you do me the honour of becoming my wife?' he said huskily. 'I want us to grow old together...have children together and fall into bed together every night from now until eternity.'

Her eyes misted with tears and she dropped down on her knees beside him to wrap her arms tightly around him. 'Just name a day and I'll be there,' she promised softly.

EPILOGUE

IT WAS early summer in Provence and sizzling hot. Caitlin walked out of the kitchen door and looked down over the garden. Thanks to the new irrigation system that had been installed, the orchard looked lush and the vines had started to bear fruit. It was delightful standing in the shade admiring the difference that the last few months had brought to Villa Mirabelle...her inheritance. There was a new red roof that glowed in the sunshine. The windows had all been replaced, their style lovingly in keeping with the period of the property. The interior was even more impressive. Polished wooden floors ran throughout and there was a superb new kitchen fitted around the trusty wood-fired stove and, what was more, the water was now properly connected to the main supply. Upstairs the bedrooms had been restored and furnished with antiques and decorated with stylish simplicity that was unique to a French country cottage.

'I think you would be pleased, Murdo,' Caitlin whispered as she watched a little bird fluttering down to sit in the almond tree. 'It is my last morning here, but Villa Mirabelle feels like a home again.'

'Caitlin?' Her mother's voice drifted out from the house. 'Caitlin, where are you? Flowers have arrived.'

Caitlin smiled. 'Oh, and I forgot to tell you. My mother is going to be living in your house…just for a while. She wants to be close by so that she can see her first grandchild.' Caitlin put her hand on her stomach, still flat as yet. 'The baby is due at the end of December, Murdo, so Christmas is going to be very busy this year. What do you think of the name Paris, by the way? I thought it was appropriate…'

'Caitlin?' Her mother appeared at the kitchen door and caught her breath in a gasp. 'Oh, darling, you look so beautiful!'

Caitlin turned. She was wearing a full-length pale gold dress that clung to her slender figure and shimmered as the sunshine caught it. Her hair was caught up on top of her head, held with fresh flowers.

'The most beautiful bride ever,' her mother said, taking out a tissue and dabbing at her eyes.

'Now, Mum, don't start blubbering just yet,' Caitlin said with a smile as she headed back towards the house.

'I can't help it,' Elaine Palmer said as she blew her nose noisily. 'I'm just so happy for you. Ray is such a wonderful man and you are both so much in love. What are you doing out here anyway?'

'Just having a few moments' quiet reflection.'

'The cars are here.' Heidi appeared behind Elaine and smiled at her friend. 'It's time to leave.'

As Caitlin stepped out of the cottage for the last time as a single woman she couldn't help but feel a pang of nostalgia. She found herself remembering the first day she had arrived here in that terrible storm and the way Ray had caught her in his arms and held her. Then she remembered the way he had proposed to her out here by the front step. And it had been here a few weeks later that she had told him about their baby.

She smiled at that memory. Ray had suggested that they wait six months before they got married. 'I think it's a good idea, Caitlin, because that way you'll know without a shadow of a doubt that this wedding has nothing to do with the terms of Murdo's will and everything to do with how much I love you.'

'I know that anyway,' she said gently. 'And I think waiting six months is a terrible idea.'

'Well, it does seem a long time away...' He shrugged.

'Yes, it does.' She smiled up at him. 'And in six months I might not be able to fit so easily into a wedding dress.'

Ray frowned at that. 'What on earth do you mean?'

'I'm pregnant, Ray. Our baby is due at Christmas.'

She remembered the look of surprise on his face, and then the intense joy. He had held her so tightly, kissed her so tenderly and the moment had been so poignant and so perfect that just thinking about it now made tears of happiness come into her eyes.

Caitlin closed the door quietly behind her. The future beckoned, a future that promised to be wonderful in every way.

MILLS & BOON® PUBLISH EIGHT LARGE PRINT TITLES A MONTH. THESE ARE THE EIGHT TITLES FOR MARCH 2005

❧

THE MISTRESS WIFE
Lynne Graham

THE OUTBACK BRIDAL RESCUE
Emma Darcy

THE GREEK'S ULTIMATE REVENGE
Julia James

THE FRENCHMAN'S MISTRESS
Kathryn Ross

THE AUSTRALIAN TYCOON'S PROPOSAL
Margaret Way

CHRISTMAS EVE MARRIAGE
Jessica Hart

THE DATING RESOLUTION
Hannah Bernard

THE GAME SHOW BRIDE
Jackie Braun

MILLS & BOON®

Live the emotion

0205 R

MILLS & BOON® PUBLISH EIGHT LARGE PRINT TITLES A MONTH. THESE ARE THE EIGHT TITLES FOR APRIL 2005

HIS PREGNANCY ULTIMATUM
Helen Bianchin

BEDDED BY THE BOSS
Miranda Lee

THE BRAZILIAN TYCOON'S MISTRESS
Fiona Hood-Stewart

CLAIMING HIS CHRISTMAS BRIDE
Carole Mortimer

TO WIN HIS HEART
Rebecca Winters

THE MONTE CARLO PROPOSAL
Lucy Gordon

THE LAST-MINUTE MARRIAGE
Marion Lennox

THE CATTLEMAN'S ENGLISH ROSE
Barbara Hannay

MILLS & BOON®

Live the emotion

0305 Rom LP